HARDPAN

a novel

MARILYN SKINNER LANIER

WESTERLY DIRECTIONS PRESS

HARDPAN

Book cover design by Matthew Silas

Book cover photograph by Quyen Tran

Published by Westerly Directions Press, 2015

FIRST EDITION

ISBN 978-0-9965372-1-6 Hardcover

ISBN 978-0-9965372-2-3 Trade Paperback

To my parents, Jim and Marcia Skinner,
for their brave optimism in the face of hardship

CONTENTS

I

Clark, Wyoming 1954

II

Badger Basin, Wyoming 1956

III

Modesto, California 1957

I

CLARK, WYOMING 1954

1

SIGNING THE LEASE

Kurt was surprised that the elevator spooked David. After all, he was almost ten and fearless. Guess he hadn't ridden in many elevators. Matter of fact, must be his first time in a genuine high-rise. You don't find high rises in places like Jordan Valley, Oregon, a town with one hundred ninety-three people if you count the baby born before Joey Seteca died last month.

He felt weary from yesterday's long drive, ten hours across the Oregon high desert, through the Columbia River Gorge and north on US 99 to reach Seattle. He rubbed his sweaty hands together, wondering about the lawyer he was about to meet. Would he offer lease terms that wouldn't require cash down? He couldn't afford to move his family again, this time all the way to Wyoming, if it involved a down payment.

He was still chafing from losing his shirt in his cousin's rock crushing business. He and Jo had worked hard to save that five thousand dollars. Went down the drain with the rock crushing business.

While rummaging for the ad from the Idaho *Daily Statesman* stuffed deep down in his pocket, the elevator doors ground open. He smoothed the rumpled ad from the Sunday paper dated February 7, 1954. "Wanted. Ranch manager for large operation in NW Wyoming. Golden opportunity for self-starter."

He spotted the blocky sign on the oak door across the hall:

"Continental Grain Company."

"There it is, Dad!" David hollered.

"Yes, sonny boy." He fidgeted again with the crumpled ad. It was his ticket to a new start, free of brotherly interference. He had cut it from the Sunday paper over a month ago.

David sprinted across the hall and shoved the oak door wide open. Caught by surprise, the young receptionist seemed startled. She stood up and waddled around her desk in high heels, different from any he'd ever seen—not the usual saddle shoes or worn huaraches favored by his mother.

"Can I help you?" she said breathlessly.

Suddenly shy, David glanced away.

Kurt stepped up. He guessed she couldn't be more than twenty-one. Her curly blonde hair dangled loosely over the collar of her red suit jacket. "Yes, ma'am. Kurt Glover here to see Mr. Whitaker."

"Oh, Mr. Glover. You're a few minutes early, aren't you?" She gazed intently at him, making Kurt wonder if his favorite blue plaid shirt and only pair of gabardine slacks weren't to her big city standards. He glanced at the fancy standing clock in the corner. The hands showed eight forty.

"Yes, looks like it. I gave myself some extra time to figure out these city streets." He smiled, but she remained expressionless.

"You'll need to wait. He's not expecting you yet."

"How about letting him know we're here anyway?"

"Okay. Soon as he's off the phone."

She peered through a slit in the door to see Whitaker barking at someone. "No. This isn't optional. It's a court order! See you there at nine tomorrow." He slammed down the phone.

The receptionist stepped gingerly inside Whitaker's office, letting the huge door close behind her. She came back minutes later, smoothing her suit jacket repeatedly as if it were rumpled.

"Is something wrong, Miss?" Kurt asked. He wondered if his

appointment was in jeopardy.

"No. Have a seat. He'll be with you in a few minutes." She pointed to the two leather chairs opposite her desk.

Kurt had barely sat down before he sprang back up and began pacing the waiting room. While the receptionist looked at pictures in *Life* magazine, he caught a glimpse of a sultry Marilyn Monroe nestled against the arm of her husband, Joe DiMaggio, one of Kurt's favorite baseball players. Photographers stormed the famous couple with flashing light bulbs. Across the room, David checked out the wall thermostat and peeked behind a heavy gilt-framed mirror to see how it attached to the wall. That's my boy, Kurt thought. Always trying to figure out how things work.

It was nine thirty, almost an hour later, when Whitaker's office door finally opened again. Mr. Whitaker strode into the room as if he owned the place. He wore a navy pinstriped suit with gold cufflinks that sparkled in the room's lamplight. Every strand of his light brown hair was slicked back. His pale blue eyes squinted, and his pasty-white face proved he hadn't recently seen the sun. He sure didn't have Kurt's thick shock of black hair, or his perpetual ruddiness.

Kurt stepped back to clear some space between them as the attorney stared down Kurt's lanky six-foot frame.

"Mr. Glover?"

"Yes, sir. Good to meet you. This is my son, David. Do you mind if he stays here with me while we talk?

David looked sideways at the fancy-dressed lawyer, studying him up and down.

"Fine by me, though this may take a while," Whitaker replied.

"I'll find something to do. Don't worry about me," David reassured him.

"Well then. Why don't we get started?" Whitaker ushered them into his office. David leaned against the wood paneled wall in the back of the room as Kurt took a seat opposite the swivel chair on the other side of the big oak desk. The desktop had only a bronze inkwell at the back and a carved, wooden tray bulging with papers placed to one side.

Far below the tall office windows, a giant, red neon sign, "Public Market Center," glistened through the fog. A foghorn periodically blared through the dense, misty air, warning car ferries that plowed across Elliott Bay of the approaching terminal.

As Mr. Whitaker pulled a stack of papers from the drawer, Kurt drew his chair closer.

"Are those the lease papers? Looks like a Sears Catalog!"

"It's mostly boilerplate. Nothing to worry about." Whitaker looked across the desk.

Kurt's throat tightened. He'd never had to sign a lease to run a ranch. "I hope this doesn't require a law degree to understand it."

"Not at all. It's my job to make sure it's all in plain English."

Kurt leaned back in his chair and stretched his long legs under the desk. "Good to know you have the legal training." He pulled out the newspaper ad again and handed it to Whitaker. "This is the ad that got my attention. Seemed like a good chance at starting my own ranch."

Whitaker shoved his chair closer to the desk and leaned toward Kurt. "You bet. It's an excellent opportunity for a man like you who already knows how to ranch."

"Yes, sir. This lease gives me a fresh start. My older brother wants me off the family ranch."

"That's harsh. Are you both living there?"

Kurt twisted in his chair. Why had he mentioned his brother? The conversation unsettled him. He didn't feel comfortable talking about Sam. Didn't want to go into family issues with an outsider.

"No. Close by, though. He's in a small town in Idaho across the state border with his wife and four children. They live a few blocks from the Texaco filling station he runs. He didn't take to running the ranch. Said it wasn't in his blood."

"So you've been running the ranch for a year?"

"No, sir. About three years now. More than that, if you count my growing up years on the ranch before the Army drafted me in '42. I could've gotten an exemption because of the family ranch, but I felt it was my duty to help out the war effort. In '46, I turned my Army uniform in for a pair of overalls and a set of earplugs to go into the rock-crushing business with my cousin in Ontario, a town in eastern Oregon. When that fell through, my folks were glad to have me back."

Mr. Whitaker shifted forward and peered closely at Kurt. "So, you've been managing the family ranch since 1951?"

"Yes, sir. I always wanted to take charge of the ranch, to help out my folks in their older years. Add to that, Jo and I sunk our savings into the rock crushing business and lost it all, our entire investment, while our family was getting bigger. David there has two younger sisters only a year apart—Linda is almost eight, and Jean close to seven." He gestured toward David, who leafed through an atlas he had pulled off the bookshelf.

"Your brother wants you off the ranch even though he's running a gas station?"

Kurt nodded. "He's nervous about me running the ranch for too long. He figures he should have all rights to it, being the oldest son and all."

Why'd he say that? He didn't want to bad-mouth his brother, though he still chafed at Sam's quirks. Sam had insisted on his entitlement to the ranch even after Mother had reminded them all that the estate would be cut four ways—among her four children—after she and Dad died. Even Anna, his younger sister, a Catholic nun pledged to a life of poverty, would receive her fair share.

"That's too bad. I've seen that happen in family businesses.

There's always one sorry bastard who wants it all for himself."

Kurt heaved a sigh. "As long as I can make a living by ranching, even in Wyoming, it'll be okay. Better than battling Sam. I can haggle over cattle rights with the BLM, but battling my older brother isn't my calling."

"I'm not an expert on cattle rights. Continental Grain is a grain and feed company. We grow feed for livestock and poultry. You may have seen our big grain elevators in Longview when you drove up yesterday."

"Matter of fact, I did."

"Anyhow, sounds like you might be willing to take some risks to get ahead?" Whitaker drew a big circle on the yellow-lined pad with his sharpened pencil.

Kurt leaned forward. "No question! I know something about taking risks. Some ventures don't pan out, like the rock crushing business. I spent our life savings buying heavy equipment that locked up in the Oregon high desert winter."

"I suppose that primed you for the challenges of ranching in Wyoming?"

"I expect so. I hear Wyoming has damned cold winters. We nearly froze our rear ends working on Oregon state highway projects in the dead of winter."

Whitaker's back stiffened. Surely, Kurt knew Wyoming winters were bitter cold, worse than Oregon's. He fiddled with his No.2 pencil, but Kurt kept talking.

"We crushed rock wherever the state wanted to repair the highway. Some God-forsaken places, I can tell you."

Kurt took a deep breath. "Now, about the Wyoming ranch. What are the cattle rights? How many acres under cultivation?"

"Never heard of cattle rights in that country. But, it's a big spread. Almost fourteen hundred acres. About half is suited for growing crops. Fields to the west of the Clarks Fork River are in alfalfa now. The land on the other side of the river is rocky, better suited to raising sheep.”

Kurt leaned back in his seat for the first time. “That should be enough acreage for cattle. Good to separate acreage for the cattle from sheep grazing fields, too. Sheep can destroy a good crop by overgrazing faster than locusts in summertime.”

“It’s an option. Up to you. However, I predict you’ll have better luck with raising cattle and sheep than growing turkeys. My company purchased the ranch from a fellow who tried to raise turkeys on it. He couldn’t make a go of it.”

Kurt squirmed in his seat. He rubbed his chin as if removing his morning stubble. What would Jo think about him signing up for a former turkey ranch, for God’s sake? She’s had to adjust to life on a cattle ranch after growing up in small Oregon towns. And Wyoming is so far away, over six hundred miles from the folks’ ranch in eastern Oregon. Thank goodness he wasn’t worried about the kids. They’ll take it in stride so long as the family stays together.

Whitaker squared the pile of lease papers. “Look. I want to be frank with you. Yes, the Wyoming winters are cold. And it can be harsh. But the previous guy messed up. Our company offers you an excellent business venture with this three-year lease. Getting a working hay ranch at the base of the Absaroka Range is rare.”

“I’m still concerned about the cattle rights. If there’s enough land.”

Whitaker scoffed at the notion. “Enough land for cattle grazing, with over twelve hundred acres? That’s not something you need to worry about. Technically, it’s a hay ranch with feedlots. You buy feeder calves in the fall and bulk them up with green chop over the winter.”

Green chop? He’d heard of it, but Oregon ranchers didn’t need to store fresh cut alfalfa in a silo over the winter to help fatten the cattle. They had plenty of hay to last the winter.

"That's a different kind of operation for me." Kurt stared at the ceiling. "But maybe not that different. I've mowed alfalfa and baled hay every summer on my folks' ranch since I was a kid." He settled back in his chair.

Whitaker smoothed his slicked-back hair. "You've got it right. This operation isn't that different from what you're used to. Let's look at the terms of the lease."

~

They talked through the terms, page by page, for the next hour. Kurt asked questions and Whitaker offered comments. At last, Kurt pushed the pile away and shoved his chair back.

"I think this could work."

Whitaker's deep voice rang out in the quiet room. "So you'll accept the terms?"

Kurt started fidgeting with the papers in front of him. "Not quite. A couple more questions."

Whitaker carefully placed his hands back on the table. "What else can I answer for you?"

"Will I have an option to renew after three years?"

"We can do that."

"Good." Kurt shifted in his chair. "Require a deposit?"

"No. Not for a multi-year lease."

Kurt heaved a sigh of relief. "My wife will be happy about that."

He paused again. "What kind of profit can I expect each year? Can you show me any business records?"

"I have some records I can show you. But they're from a turkey operation. It doesn't bear much resemblance to a hay ranch."

Kurt poked holes in one of the pages with his pen. He was getting nervous about the transaction. It seemed odd that Whitaker didn't have any records for the hay ranch. "How do you figure we can make a profit then?"

Whitaker bored into him. "No question, you can! There are plenty of hay ranchers in that valley who make a good living. You know all about bulking up cattle over the winter and selling them to market."

Kurt's voice got gravelly. He didn't like this lawyer hurrying him to sign the lease. "That may be true, but it's my family. I've got to make the right decision here."

He kept coming back to Jo. She never questioned his decisions when it came to ranching. But she'd been through a lot already with his being overseas in the war during most of her first two pregnancies, and losing their savings on their first business venture after he got out of the Army in '46. Important that she feels good about this new business venture. They were both in their early thirties now, raising a family, and just getting by.

Whitaker placed the lease papers in front of him again. "I understand that. You're right to be cautious, but you'd be a fool to miss this opportunity."

Kurt shifted his weight on the chair. "You could be right."

"Any other questions?" Whitaker asked.

"No, sir. Seems like you've answered them."

"Let's get your signature on the line." He dipped the fountain pen into the inkwell and handed it to Kurt.

Kurt was still uneasy about signing the lease. But Whitaker *had* answered all his questions. After all, this move would take him in the right direction. If he and Jo worked hard enough over the next three years, they could build up enough savings to buy their own ranch.

His hand shook as he signed and dated the document, *"Kurt William Glover, March 12, 1954."* He handed the pen back to Whitaker. It was almost eleven o'clock when they finished. They stepped back from the table and shook hands.

Kurt stretched his arms behind his back, his muscles tight

from the long session. He glimpsed at David who stood in front of the tall windows, staring at the city street scene below.

"Let's go home, Son."

~

The trip home dragged on. He'd driven over three hundred miles already. It felt longer than the trip out. Once he took the ninety-degree turn east on the outskirts of Bend, he'd be on the home stretch with another two hundred seventy miles to go. David nestled beside him, already sound asleep.

He congratulated himself on having signed the ranch lease. Not bad for a day's work, he thought. But he couldn't shake a nagging thought about Wyoming. Could he make a go of a place he hadn't seen yet? What if it didn't work out? Soon he'd be letting everyone know his plans to move off the ranch. You never know. Sam might be relieved. Maybe he'd feel less threatened.

Anyway, Mother had already given her blessing. He had been cautious when he first approached her.

"You're sure about this, Mother? Who can help manage the ranch after I'm gone?"

"I'm sure we can find a local man, maybe one of the Holts, who'd like some supplemental income. Don't count your father out either. He's still able-bodied, you know."

"Yep. He sure is, but if I go through with this lease, I'll be sure someone is ready to help you and Dad."

She hugged him tight. "Thanks, Son. I'm pleased this will give you a fresh start. Could be your first step toward owning your own ranch!"

~

At midnight, he pulled into the driveway of the rock house. Jo was waiting up for them. "Did you sign the lease?" she asked quietly.

"Sure did. Now it's up to us. You and I know all about hard work, what it takes to make a living. The terms are good."

Gripped by the details, and comforted by his easy optimism, Jo listened to Kurt. It seemed like yesterday that they had made the difficult decision to abandon his rock crushing business after losing their investment. Five thousand dollars gone so quick. But they had moved to the family ranch over three years ago with three young children in tow. She set aside her worries and wrapped her arms around him. She loved his fighting spirit. He was good at bouncing back when he hit a wall.

"We can do it, honey," she said. "It'll be good for you to head your own ranch operation. No family members to interfere."

She surprised him. He knew she meant Sam, but she was being sensitive to his desire not to confront his older brother.

~

Before going to bed, he waited while Jo let in Mr. Brown, the family mutt. She tossed David's dirty clothes into the hamper on the back porch outside the bathroom door. At last, she followed Kurt into their bedroom. He slipped out of his Levis as she pulled her red silky nightgown over her head. The gown had been a Christmas present from Kurt, and she felt sexy wearing it. They slid next to each other in the double bed.

"Let's aim for moving in April. It'll give us time to become acquainted with the ranch before the haying season starts."

"What? That's only a month away. The kids will still be in school."

"Yeah, I know. But it won't hurt them, they're smart kids."

Jo took time to reply. Kurt knew Linda was doing fine in school, but David lagged behind in reading. A couple of times lately, she'd said the teacher reported that he wasn't reading well. Each time, Kurt said the same thing. "Don't worry, honey. He's a smart boy. He'll pick up on reading. You just watch."

His casual reaction to David's reading problems annoyed her. At the same time, it was true David could distinguish between every model of tractor on the ranch, and with a little help from Kurt, he figured out how to use the foot clutch and hand throttle on the John Deere Model A. In fact, he preferred driving the tractor in the fields to reading his schoolbooks. But she knew he needed schoolbook learning, even if he became a rancher like his dad. The business of running a ranch was becoming more complex every day.

Kurt gazed at her. "You worrying about David again?"

She grimaced. Kurt could read her pretty well. "Yes. You know he's behind Linda on his reading skills."

"He'll catch up. A new teacher could be a good thing." He paused.

She nodded reluctantly. "Maybe a few weeks won't make a big difference."

He breathed a sigh of relief, and moved on. "Alright then. I don't want to leave the folks empty-handed. I'll arrange for the first haying to be done by the Eiguren boys. Dad can supervise."

"If the Eiguren boys can help their father get his fields done first, that'll work. Jack will be glad to return the favor. Remember how you helped him when Elda got sick last year?" Jo offered.

"Yep."

Her mind wandered back to the move. "Do you suppose we can get all our furniture into one truck?"

"I doubt it, but the folks won't mind if we leave some furniture behind. And we won't need to take a lot of equipment. Whitaker said the Wyoming ranch has some basic machinery —tractors and mowers—stored in the barn. The big challenge will be getting Chestnut into a horse trailer. He's twelve hands tall, and he must weigh a thousand pounds. I'll see if we can buy Duncan's trailer. He might even give it to me. He never uses it, and it should be big enough. Mr. Brown can ride with him."

"Good thing that Chestnut is used to having the mutt around him. They'll get to know each other real well over the two-day trip!" They laughed.

Their conversation gradually faded away. Jo snuggled alongside him. Before long, their slow breathing filled the quiet of the small bedroom.

2

JO

The wind came from Line Creek Canyon without warning, leaving only a pretense of soil in its wake. The locals called it hardpan: soil so hard even sagebrush couldn't grow in it.

Kurt and Jo leaned together to stay upright. The afternoon winds roared easterly from the canyon past the ranch house on the bank of the Clarks Fork River. The faded white two-story frame house stood in stubborn isolation on the silty riverbank. Persistent winds and unforgiving sun had ravaged the coats of white paint applied over the years.

"What do you think?" He pressed her for an answer. Their moving truck was still full of furniture and boxes.

She tucked her sleeveless, white cotton shirt into her dusty blue pedal pushers, struggling to keep her clothes intact as the wind gusted around her. Strands of her reddish-blonde hair blew across her face, sticking to her lips. She brushed the hair away and licked back and forth across her mouth to make the wetness stick.

"It's not what I expected." She grimaced at the peeling strands of paint dangling from the window frames. The house looked like it hadn't been painted in years. "Do you think some fresh paint can bring it back to life?"

He was caught unawares. It wasn't what he expected either, but leave it to Jo to notice these kinds of details. He hadn't thought much about the house until now. He'd spent time checking out the equipment stored in the barn instead. He studied the house again, this time in earnest, and concluded Jo was right. It *was* shabby. "You bet, honey. We can paint the place." He thumped his chest with his fist in his cheerful bullyboy way, and she rewarded him with a wispy smile, her lips thin as cirrus clouds before an approaching storm.

It felt like they had landed on the moon after their two-day drive from eastern Oregon. Back home, they had never painted their house. No need to paint a rock house. Only the front porch required a fresh coat from time-to-time.

"Your hat!"

"What?"

"Your hat!" she shouted into his ear, pointing toward the river below.

They watched his best Stetson catapult to the riverbed some thirty feet below. By the time it reached the stream, it was only a brown speck tossed against piles of boulders and river rock as the water thrashed its way to the Yellowstone River.

"Too late, honey." He couldn't believe his favorite hat was gone just like that. Taken by a gust of wind. He couldn't replace it with another Stetson anytime soon. Too expensive. One of his baseball caps would have to do. Any extra cash would have to go toward fixing up the house and updating their ranch vehicles— some of them appeared to be on their last legs.

The mighty Absaroka Range towered ten thousand feet above the river and the vast expanses of sagebrush and cultivated fields in the Clarks Fork Valley below. The ranch was one of a dozen in the valley. Outfits sparsely distributed on either side of the river looked like tiny spots of civilization in the remote landscape.

A weathered barn and chicken coop stood near the ranch

house, both structures permanently tilted by Wyoming's trademark winds. Across the lane, the screen door of the bunkhouse flapped incessantly, attached only by a single bracket on the upper left side.

~

One afternoon in late April, Kurt sprayed the alfalfa field with fertilizer while Jo watched from the garden. The weathered frame bunkhouse loomed behind her. Pale green, the fields held the promise of spring as far as the eyes could see. Hundreds of acres of fields, first planted years ago, stretched west to the foothills of the Rockies.

Kurt idled the John Deere along the edge of the field and hopped down, taking his usual long, fast strides to reach her. He kicked the ground with the toe of his boot to dislodge some clods. "It's early enough in the season; a good spraying of fertilizer should help. I'm hoping to get two to three cuttings this summer."

"Do you think the haying season here is shorter than in Oregon? Those huge mountains behind us are the Rockies, you know. I've heard it can snow on the passes as early as the 4th of July!"

"We'll see. Don't let those mountains intimidate you. This valley isn't much higher than Jordan Valley. Around forty-five hundred feet elevation. And you know how people exaggerate about the weather."

"Let's hope so. Better for us to have a longer growing season." He was always so resolute in the face of daunting challenges. Reminded her of when he crushed rock in the freezing cold of winter back home in Oregon.

He tossed her the tractor key. "Here you go. It's all yours. Jump up there."

"You know I don't drive tractors!" She had resisted his attempts to teach her how to drive the tractors. She had enough to do running the household, growing a garden, and taking care of the kids.

"Don't worry. I'll help you. I've got to drive to Powell for some replacement parts."

He swatted her on the behind, laughing as she swung onto the tractor seat.

"You look good up there!"

"I don't see the pedal," she said, shading her eyes from the sun.

"It doesn't have one. Look for the hand throttle, a short little handle, on your right."

"I got it."

"Put it in gear and give it some gas. Pull back on the throttle to get power." She felt her face flush. So many orders! Sometimes he forgot she wasn't one of the kids. The noisy diesel engine drowned out his voice, and Jo took off before he finished giving directions.

He watched as the tractor lurched through the bumpy field, spraying behind as it moved forward. He knew she could do it!

"Jo!" he shouted. "Speed it up. The wind's whipping the fertilizer onto your back."

She glanced down at her sleeves damp from the spray of chemicals. "Too late," she yelled back to him. "It got me already. Guess this is my baptism into Wyoming ranching!"

"You're doing great!" Kurt waved her forward with a grin wide as the riverbed. She turned back and smiled in return.

A few sprinkles from the tractor spray thrust her into a whole new world governed by unexpected forces of nature. It reminded her of her baptism into the Catholic faith days before their marriage in '43. A few sprinkles of water on her forehead by the priest meant she and Kurt could be married in Saint John's Cathedral.

Just like that, she became part of his family's religious tradition. She never regretted her decision to convert. It was a good way to break the ties with a Baptist mother who had abandoned her when Jo was still a child.

~

As he strode back toward the house, a car pulled to a stop next to the bunkhouse. A couple, looking around the same age as Kurt and Jo, got out of the Nash Rambler.

"Mr. Glover?"

"Yes. It's Kurt."

"Tom Kowalski. My wife, Irene."

Kurt gripped Tom's hand and flashed Irene his most charming smile.

Tom stood about five feet six, a solid block of muscle framed by broad shoulders. Chapped from the wind and the sun, his cheeks were a weathered red. His squinty eyes matched the blue in Kurt's plaid shirt and faded Levis.

Tom's wife was nearly her husband's height, but thin and wiry as a coat hanger. Her flowery cotton dress looked straight off a JCPenney's rack. She grabbed Kurt's hand and shook it hard.

"Good to meet you. I see your wife out there spraying. I bet she gets her ass wet!" Her belly laugh filled the air as she peered across the field to get another glimpse of Jo on the tractor.

Jo chuckled when Kurt told her about the incident later that evening. "No kidding! She *really* said that? I've got to meet her."

"You bet. She invited us over. Said we're welcome anytime."

~

On her way into town later that week, Jo stopped by the Kowalski ranch. She had looked forward to this visit with Irene. She missed her friends in eastern Oregon, especially Pearl, her hairdresser friend, who always insisted Jo stick around for a late afternoon chat before she rushed home to fix dinner for her family.

She missed Minnie, too. Minnie and her husband ran the town's only grocery store. She was a real character. Every room of her house was filled with stacks of used paperbacks and out-of-control children. She smoked like a chimney and played cards with Jo and her friends while telling raunchy stories that made Jo blush.

When Irene opened the front door, the smell of urine drifted out, overwhelming Jo. She figured the boys must be bed-wetters.

Irene waved her inside. "Come on in."

Jo caught sight of a large oak barrel in the center of the living room. The threadbare sofa and equally worn armchair had been shoved against the wall to make space for it.

"What do you have in there?" Jo asked. She wondered if the stink wasn't the kids, after all.

"Sauerkraut. That barrel's pert near full. With my big family, it will be empty in no time." Irene paused proudly over the barrel before swinging back to the kitchen to get coffee.

Jo's suspicion was confirmed. The fermenting cabbage created that stink. She exonerated the boys, though she could see their disorganized bedroom a few feet away. Bed sheets and blankets draped loosely to the floor. T-shirts, Levi's, and dirty socks were scattered everywhere. The mess wasn't to her standards. She liked things to be orderly. Kurt teased her about how she always kept the house clean. He knew how important it was to her.

"Want some?" Irene handed her a chipped, white ceramic mug of fresh brew.

"Yes, thanks," Jo said, grateful for the familiar aroma. She sat beside Irene on the sofa and sipped the coffee.

"I'm still wondering if you got your ass wet on your John Deere that day. Your husband didn't say much when I asked him during our visit last week."

"Guess you caught him by surprise. He had warned me about catching the spray if I didn't drive faster, but it was too late. I got soaked!"

Irene laughed. "Bet you'll throttle down harder next time!"

Jo nodded. "No doubt."

They laughed together. The conversation got easier after that.

~

Kurt and Jo got through their first haying season intact. Not many surprises except for the occasional flash floods from Line Creek that ripped out the canvas dams that Kurt, sometimes with David's help, put in place in the ditches to divert water to the fields.

Irrigation was tricky business. During haying season, Kurt hired a full-time irrigator to yank out the canvas dams and reset them a hundred feet or so upstream, repeating the cycle many times a day. With rubber boots up to his knees, he used his shovel to dig holes into the ditch bank and toss glops of mud on either side to hold the canvas in place.

For sandy soil, he placed semi-circular siphons near the top of the ditch bank to make an outlet for the water. With so many fields under cultivation, hundreds of dams were set and reset all season long.

Although it took Jo awhile to become accustomed to using the foot treadle on her Singer sewing machine, she improved at making the canvas dams. The machine virtually hummed when she fed huge sheets of white canvas through the feeder, both feet planted squarely on the treadle.

Her mother-in-law had given her the reliable old machine before she and Kurt left for Wyoming. She'd be pleased to know Jo used it to make the canvas dams that provided a measure of protection from the torrential water that ran downstream from the mountains during summer thunderstorms, threatening to wipe out the ditches.

~

Kurt figured there was enough baled hay to feed the cattle through the coming winter. Money from the summer hay crop and the steers he'd taken to market would pay the bills and hopefully, leave enough to make the first year's lease payment due the following June. And he'd managed to set aside some cash to purchase about fifty head of sheep that autumn from a fellow in Belfry. Things were going pretty damned well.

3

MEAL TICKET FOR SURVIVAL

Linda peeked at the icy windowpane from a pile of covers. "Sissy! Let's go downstairs. It's freezing up here."

Jean squirmed on her side of the bed. "You first!"

Clad in flannel pajamas and cotton socks, the two girls slid across the smooth pine planks toward the stairwell, skidding to a halt outside David's room.

Linda cracked his door open. "You awake?"

"Go away. Gotta get some sleep." He scooted deeper beneath the mountain of army blankets. "Dad and I were up late watching ewes."

"Did they drop any lambs?"

"Not one! Dad says they're ready, but nothing happened."

A shaft of sunlight from the frosty, east window crossed his bed.

"Oh, my gosh, David. You've got snow on your bed," Linda said. "It looks like powdered sugar!"

He poked his head above the covers and swept his finger across the thin layer of snow, licking it like a lollipop. "Wind must have blown the snow through cracks in the window frame. Those ewes are better off than I am."

The girls giggled. Jean scooted to his bedside and tugged at his arm. "Come downstairs. You're awake now."

"All right. You two get going. I'll be down in a minute."

The girls trailed down the narrow staircase to the kitchen. A rush of warm air welcomed them as they burst into the room. Kurt had stoked the big coal furnace in the living room with extra coal before going to bed, expecting outside temperatures to drop overnight to twenty below zero with the wind chill.

Linda peeked into their parents' bedroom. "Hey!" she whispered. "You awake?"

"We are now," Kurt mumbled. "Good morning, seagulls."

David elbowed past his sisters. "Morning, Dad."

Kurt blinked. "Thought you'd sleep in."

David shrugged. "These two wouldn't let me."

"Stop it! It's freezing up there. Your bed is covered with snow!" Jean said.

"I'm not surprised," Kurt said. "When we walked back last night, the blizzard blew us sideways."

"Yeah. My face got pummeled," David added.

Jo pulled her arms outside the covers. "You've had quite a night, honey. Is there really snow on your bed?"

"Yep. You can check for yourself. I didn't feel it though, 'cause I was under a pile of blankets."

Jo grinned at him. "That's good. I'm glad you stayed warm after all that." She pulled herself up against the headboard to sit next to Kurt.

"Did you know your dad found twin lambs after you went to bed?" She winked at Kurt. "Right, honey?"

"Really, Dad? After we watched 'em all night and nothing happened?" David's low voice gave away his disappointment.

"Yep. These things are unpredictable. You kids better go check on those lambs. Make sure the ewe is tending them," Kurt replied.

"Bundle up! It's below zero out there," Jo warned.

When the children were safely gone, Jo hugged Kurt. "Thanks for going along with me on that, honey. We could use some more sleep."

He chuckled. "You never know. They may find a lamb or two. Those ewes' bellies almost touch the ground."

Minutes later the children rushed through their bedroom door.

"We found 'em," Linda squealed. "But one's stiff as a board. The ewe didn't finish licking him."

"Yep. Only one alive, Dad," David said. "The ewe is still in the holding pen."

Kurt reached for his Levis. "Come with me, Son. You can help me move the ewe and her lamb into the shed. We've got to start manning the lookout, too."

He had built a tiny lookout above the main shed that they manned 24/7 during peak lambing season. Dug into the hillside above the river, the woodshed protected the ewes and their new-born lambs from the frigid air above ground. Four-by-four cubicles formed two long rows. Each could hold two or three ewes and their lambs.

When Kurt and David got to the shed, they worked fast to move any ready-to-drop ewes from the fenced-in holding pen to the warm indoors. It took only minutes for a newborn lamb's slimy skin to freeze. The ewe could barely lick him off in February temperatures that often hovered at twenty below zero.

Bred to deliver late winter, the ewes gave birth to the lambs so the ranchers could go to early market in the fall. Like other ranchers in the Clark Valley, Kurt had to weigh the risks of lambing during the winter months against the advantages of hitting the market early for better prices.

When Kurt returned to the house in the late afternoon, traces of snow lined his thick eyebrows. The cold had reddened his nose and cheeks. He draped a lamb over his right arm, its spindly legs dangling mid-air, and placed it in the cardboard box set up next to the stove in the living room. Jo had layered the box with newspapers and some straw from the barn.

"Here you go, Jo. A bummer. He's weak. Needs some warm milk. We lost the ewe in the outside pen before we could get her to the shed. She fell from her own weight, big belly and all, shaking from the wind chill. We got her lamb out, but couldn't save her. It's damned cold out there. David and I cut the cord and wrapped him in that big towel."

Jo sighed. Since arriving in this rugged country, she had learned how bummer lambs were either orphaned when the ewe died during delivery, or rejected by their mother who was too weak to care for more than one newborn. Caring for the bummers brought back memories of her own troubled childhood.

Jo's mother gave birth to five children before she turned thirty. This unwanted, heavy load must have been the reason she decided to leave Jo and her siblings to fend for themselves before Jo had started high school. Sometime before moving north with a new husband and without her children, she divorced Jo's father and admitted him to the state mental hospital in Salem because he was increasingly weak and his body shook uncontrollably. She claimed he had some sort of mental illness. She must have been unaware he had early signs of Parkinson's, a degenerative neurological disease.

Jo felt toughened by that experience. She was determined to stick by Kurt and the kids no matter what adversity befell them.

"Poor thing! I'll get a bottle ready." She filled a glass bottle with milk from the fridge and put it in a saucepan of hot water on the stove.

Jo beckoned Linda just as she stuck her spoon into a bowl of hot oatmeal. "I'm going to need your help."

"You mean while you give him a shot?" She cringed at the thought of holding a wriggling lamb while her mother stuck him with that long needle. It reminded her of the time that Johnny Gottfried had wriggled when the visiting nurse tried to give him a tetanus shot at school. The whole class heard him squeal as the needle pierced the skin on his arm.

"No shot this time. He's hungry, and you're going to learn how to feed him yourself. Here you go." Jo handed her the tall, glass bottle with an elongated black nipple. "Hold him under his belly so he can stand up while you feed him. Hold on tight or he'll pull the nipple off."

The lamb wobbled on his spindly legs, latched onto the nipple, and started sucking as Linda steadied herself. She held tight as the lamb rooted for milk, his little tail whirling as fast as he drank. He tugged at the nipple so hard it nearly came off the bottle.

"There isn't a drop left," Linda exclaimed. She patted the lamb on its head. "Good for you, little fella. You're going to make it."

They kept the lamb indoors for another day of feedings, until he was strong enough to go back to the shed. Linda named him "Spindly" and accompanied her father when he returned the little lamb to his soon-to-be adopted mother. She watched as Kurt draped the bummer with the skin from the lamb that had died during delivery.

"He'll be fine, honey," he said reassuringly. "This ewe will accept Spindly as her own because she recognizes the scent of her dead lamb."

～

At times that winter, there were three or four bummer lambs in cardboard boxes in the living room. It was their refuge from the winter storms and their meal ticket to survival.

4

SPRING REPAIRS

Determined to dodge chunks of hardpan broken loose from the spring thaw, Kurt pulled the steering wheel hard to the right.

"Oh, no. Not another repair," he muttered. "Can't afford to lose another tire to road hazards on this stretch." But Jo hadn't heard him. Just as well, he thought. Times are tough enough. No need to add to her worries.

The cab got quiet again as the pickup rumbled down the road to Powell, the silence broken only by the kids jostling for elbow-room on the crowded bench seat.

"Can we get some marbles, Mommy?" Jean asked.

"We'll see. We're going to stock up on groceries first."

"Need any more canvas for dams?" Kurt asked.

"I could use a few more rolls. Flash floods ripped most of the ones I made last summer."

Kurt nodded. "Yep. The weather can turn so fast. When I see those black thunderclouds, I hustle back to the house."

"There were a few times you didn't make it. As Irene would say, you got your ass wet."

Kurt laughed, and the kids giggled.

"Did you remember the help wanted sign?" Kurt asked.

"Yes, I've got it. Let's stop at the Job Services Office on the way into town so we can post it."

Men drawn to the region for summer employment, often with

only a bedroll and a duffel bag, studied the notices posted by local ranchers on the bulletin board. Drifters from unnamed places came after the spring thaw to find work as hired hands for the brief haying season that, in good weather years, started in late June.

Kurt glanced down on David's curly mass of dark brown hair. "Sure. We only need two men this season, what with David getting big enough to drive a tractor on his own. You gonna help me mow this year, sonny boy?"

"'Course, Dad," he beamed.

It felt good to have David as his right-hand man, though he still needed a stack of pillows on the front seat of the pickup to see over the steering wheel. He wanted his son to have the same ranch upbringing he'd had back in Oregon.

~

After loading the pickup bed with fifty-pound sacks of flour and pinto beans, box bottoms crammed with canned vegetables, and large plastic bags of breakfast cereal, Kurt stopped at the feed store on the outskirts of town. While he and David got dog food for Mr. Brown, Jo looked for grain for the chickens. The girls wandered the aisles in search of something they had to have.

"Hey, Mommy!" Jean hollered. "Look at these cute little chicks!"

Jo gazed down at the yellow pack bustling around their makeshift wire pen. Floodlights warmed the bed of loose hay.

"Can we get some?" Jean asked. She and Linda poked each other, looking hopeful.

"Now, girls. We already have four hens and Nasty. And, Jean, you'd rather have these chicks than new marbles?"

"Yes. We'll take care of them. Promise!"

Jo finally relented. "Okay. A half-dozen. No more."

The girls jumped up and down, but Jo knew the girls' enthusiasm would last only as long as the chicks' fluffy feathers.

~

On the return home, on the outskirts of town, trim front lawns facing the main road abruptly gave way to sweeping open prairie. A few miles farther, the road dropped off the bench toward the Clarks Fork Valley below. It gradually straightened its course, moving like a roller coaster up and down barren hills before reaching the wide expanse of valley.

The Absarokas loomed in the distance, casting a giant, late afternoon shadow over the western part of the valley. The mountains dwarfed the Clark's Fork Valley floor far below where the family was crammed together in the pickup cab, their spring purchases weighing down the back.

Whump! Kurt grabbed the steering wheel with both hands as the pickup dipped down on the driver's side and ground to a stop. David's head slammed into the metal dashboard. Jo and Jean piled on his back as Linda shrieked, "Our stuff is everywhere!" Boxes, canned goods, and long rolls of canvas were strewn across the road.

Linda spotted a clump of fluffy feathers wedged between two big flour sacks that had toppled to the ground.

"Our baby chicks!" she cried.

"What's the matter?" Kurt growled as he caught a glimpse of David's bruised forehead.

"Daddy, get them out!" Linda pleaded.

"Gotta tend to your brother first." He pulled David back by his shirt. "You all right, Son?"

David rubbed his forehead. "I banged my head pretty hard." He waved his bloodied fingers in the air.

Jo gasped. "You've got a gash on your forehead!" She yanked

her kerchief off her neck. "Here. Press this against your head while I tie the ends."

She surprised herself sometimes at how inventive she had become when her kids got hurt in this godforsaken place. Kurt depended on her to clean up the wounds and apply medicine and Band-Aids.

Kurt peeled back the kerchief to have a look. "Doesn't look too bad. Keep some pressure on it. Nice of you to cushion your sisters." David gave him his aw-shucks grin.

Kurt noticed Jo's eyes glistened in the late afternoon light. He patted her knee. "You okay, honey?"

"A little shaken, aren't we girls?" She clutched them beside her.

"The chicks, Daddy! They're squished in your new shoebox between the flour sacks. Everything toppled out."

Kurt shoved the door open and jumped down. "I'll get them. Not sure what I hit. You girls stay here with your mother."

"But, Dad. I can help," David insisted. He yanked the bloodied kerchief from his forehead and handed it to his mother.

"Okay, Son. Let's see what's going on." Kurt bent down to inspect the area around the damaged front tire. "It's a deep pothole. We're damned lucky I wasn't going any faster. Front tire's a goner though. Ripped clear through. You can help loosen the lug bolts, and I'll jack up the truck."

"But, Dad. The chicks." Linda pointed them out again.

Kurt and David strode to the rear of the truck and saw cargo from the spring shopping trip scattered up and down the roadside and into the ditch. Kurt reached down and manhandled a flour sack off the crushed shoebox filled with downy feathers. No sign of life there. He didn't want to share the news just yet. He knew the girls would be heart-broken.

"Are they okay, Daddy?" Linda's insistent, high-pitched voice rang out in the cool, springtime air. Jean gaped at her father, waiting for his verdict.

"Doesn't look good, honey. We'll have to get you some more chicks our next trip to town."

The girls' expressions said it all. Their precious cargo was dead. Gone. Linda knew there wasn't a thing they could do. She shivered uncontrollably. She and Jean had been so excited about those little chicks.

Kurt and David picked up the goods, shook off the road dirt, and reloaded the truck bed without the chicks. Linda stared at the mangled heap of yellow fluff left alongside the road and peered up at her dad. "Can we hold a little ceremony for the chicks? You could dig a grave for them with your shovel in the back."

Kurt winced. He felt pressure to get back on the road, but the girls looked so sad. "Alright. As soon as David and I have changed the tire, we'll get that done for you."

Jo and the girls formed a semi-circle around Kurt and David while they pulled the spare tire from the truck bed and started the tire change. Dust devils danced around the pickup from the afternoon wind, but no cars came from either direction. When Kurt tightened the last bolt, he pulled the bench seat forward and put the jack and lug wrench back into the toolbox.

"Okay, the spare looks good. David, can you hand me the shovel?" Within minutes, a little hole not much bigger than a small cardboard box was ready for the bundle of dead chicks. The girls held hands while Linda said a prayer that was difficult to hear through the whistle of the afternoon breeze. Kurt broke up the reverie.

"Okay, kids. Get in. Let's get going."

The girls trudged alongside the pickup to the door Jo held open. Inside the cab, David whispered to Kurt as he dabbed his forehead with the rag he had used to grip the lug bolts. "Glad it was only a flat tire, Dad. Could've been worse."

~

It was a few days after their trip to Powell and early morning, when Linda walked toward the dust erupting from the open barn door. She found her father shaking rolls of barbed wire pulled from a tall stack in the far corner of the barn. The rolls hadn't been touched since last fall's harvest.

"Can I go with you today, Dad?"

"No, honey." He grabbed a hammer worn smooth by years of repairing fences and fixing fallen sheds. "We've got a lot of work to do to get these fences fixed, and you need to help your mother."

Linda watched him toss the barbed wire bales onto the bed of "Jimmy," his '52 half-ton, yellow and black pickup. He stepped on the running board to reach the bales with his long, muscular arms, carefully arranging them over the fence posts on the bottom of the pickup bed.

Linda felt good that things were getting fixed again. Her father repaired broken fences and her mother made new canvas dams for the irrigation ditches. The sheep and cattle would soon be let out of the corrals and sheds to graze the fields.

The earth smelled good again, too. After months of dry, cold air and lifeless, frozen fields, the air reeked of damp grasses swollen by moisture released from melting snow. She even appreciated the stink of alfalfa silage emitting gasses again under the warm, spring sun.

5

HIRED MAN HIGH JINKS

It was getting towards midnight, late even for a Friday night. Linda, David, and Jo kept their cards face down until Kurt finished dealing the Pinochle deck.

"Hope these are better than the last hand you dealt, Dad!" Linda said.

He grunted and gazed away from the kitchen table.

Linda sensed his distraction. "Are you worried that Pike won't return your pickup?"

Earlier that evening, Kurt had announced that one of the hired men had taken Jimmy, his favorite pickup. "Nope. The keys were in the ignition, like always. I've never had to worry about a hired hand taking one of our vehicles off the ranch without asking."

"But it's Pike! Do you really expect he'll bring it back? He's not as perfect as you think. Just last night he told me that he'd like to take your pickup for a spin."

"He did?"

"Yeah. I told him that's your favorite truck and he'd better not take it. Besides, he's mean to Jean and me. He teases us about how bad we look. Makes me mad when he points out the gap between my front teeth or when he calls Jean, 'Chubbykins'."

"Now, honey. He means well. He's just not used to being around young girls."

Kurt never seemed bothered by Pike's jokes. Matter of fact,

he took to Pike almost from the first day he arrived. Pike was the first man out of the bunkhouse every morning—ready to take on any job Kurt assigned him. He never complained. He was a stocky kid from Nebraska with shoulders as broad as the planks on the bunkhouse floor, close to twenty years old. His curly red hair was as unruly as Nasty's rooster feathers. Like the other hired men, he never said much about himself or explained why he came from so far away to work on a ranch in Wyoming.

"No, honey, he'll bring it back. He can't go far. Everyone knows it's my truck. They can spot the yellow cab and black fender a mile away. But Pike may have to fix a flat tire. That rear tire was low last time I looked."

Kurt chuckled, pleased with his assessment of the situation, and the kids laughed. Jo sat quietly, pressing her forearms on the table. She couldn't believe Kurt could be so trusting. He depended on that pickup every single day to get him to and from places on both sides of the river.

David's face lit up. "Yeah, Dad. I can see him getting part way to town before discovering he has a flat tire. Maybe it'll blow out. That's what he deserves!"

Jo winced. "Now, David. We don't wish him any harm. We only want him to return your dad's truck."

She stared across the table at Kurt.

"Kurt, you don't know Pike that well. Even if he has to fix a flat tire, he could take off with your pickup for good. It's Friday night. I bet the cash you gave him after work today is burning a hole in his pocket."

Kurt seemed lost in thought. He didn't see any reason to worry about Pike returning the truck. Kurt liked to tease him. He was all of five foot seven in cowboy boots, and about two hundred pounds of solid muscle.

Kurt finally answered Jo. "I know you're worried. But he's gonna return that truck. He's a good kid. I remember taking

Dad's truck out of town to a dance when I was eighteen and having to walk home at four in the morning after I blew out the front tires on a cattle guard. Dad woke me up at six to do chores. It's a lesson that has stuck with me."

David groaned. "Oh, Dad. You're only seeing one side of this guy. Pike told me how his folks kicked him out after high school for making too much trouble. I figured it must have something to do with his temper, red hot like the color of his hair. We've all learned to steer clear of saying things like how short he is compared to other hired hands, or why he doesn't know how to saddle a horse."

And Pike sure knew how to pick a fight. One morning, Kurt had to pull him off Bob Marney after Pike had taunted Bob one time too many about having cowgirl skills. Bob was a local boy, three years older than David, who helped them out year-round on the ranch. Bob threw Pike a sucker punch and Pike struck back, gashing Bob's right cheekbone pretty bad. Blood splashed all over Jo's yellow gingham kitchen curtains.

Even so, Kurt insisted Pike was a hard worker who kept his nose to the grindstone most of the time. But this truck incident was a twist he hadn't expected.

"You know, Pike said he had a ride into town with one of the other hired men, a man named Jake—he never gave his last name. I believed him until I heard the engine turn over. Slow start at first, then full throttle down the lane."

Jo's worry lines returned.

"This isn't a good time to have your truck stolen, Kurt. Not when our crop yield is so low. Not when the land is so dry you can see cracks in the soil."

"Come on, Jo. No need to bring up our troubles. We've never had a hired man take our vehicles for more than a short ride. Not once. They've plowed through irrigation ditches and banged up some fence posts, but they've always returned the vehicles. This'll be no different."

Jo sat there, quiet, her body tight with anxiety.

Linda twisted her head around to see her father. She shrugged her shoulders. "I don't think so, Daddy."

She returned to the cards. "Two fifty!" she shouted, opening the bid for the first time that evening. She drummed the table to get their attention.

David picked up his hand. "Let's see what I got."

He and Linda won the game and a couple more after that. By one o'clock, only a few popcorn kernels were in the ceramic mixing bowl.

"Okay kids. Game's over. Time for bed," Jo said.

The three children charged up the narrow staircase from the kitchen, skipping every other step until they reached the upper landing. The rustling upstairs soon quieted down, leaving their parents time to themselves.

~

Saturday morning, the thunderclouds formed earlier than usual. It was beastly hot. The crickets swarmed low over the rows of mowed alfalfa, making a racket across the field.

David steered the dusty John Deere tractor past the freshly mowed grass onto the next field. He geared down to thread the tractor slowly through the tall grass that waved lazily in the warm breeze. Determined to reach the cluster of beehives at the edge of the field, David tried not to stir up much dust.

Before leaving the house that morning, his father had advised him about bees. "They won't bother you unless you disturb them, Son. Keep yourself covered. You'd better wear that headgear when you lift the top off the box."

David checked out the wire mesh helmet used by beekeepers. "Yeah, Dad. I get it."

"One more thing. You have to move fast when that top is off. When you reach in for a frame, grab it quick. Don't worry about getting more than one. Then run like hell back to your tractor."

As he got closer to the edge of the field, he couldn't see the boxes of beehives that were supposed to be there. He edged the tractor a few feet closer, leaning over the left side to spot the hives.

"Yikes!" he yelled into the empty field. The front wheels had rammed the hives. One box split open; the honey spread like goo over the broken box. The remnants crunched under his tires. Bees swarmed his tractor.

He reached for his helmet and frantically tried to pull it over his head. As he jerked it down, it flipped behind him onto the ground. The bees descended on his neck and face, stinging him all over.

David put his tractor on full-throttle and headed straight for the ranch house, bees swarming behind him.

"Mom!" he screamed and pushed the front door open. "I got stung!"

Jo rushed from the kitchen, recoiling in horror at the sight of David's swollen face and neck. It was blotchy with red and white rings.

"Good God! What happened?"

"I rammed the hive."

"Your face is all puffy. Sit down there. I'll be right back." She hurried to the kitchen to make a poultice with baking soda. When she returned with a wet towel in one hand and a bowl of baking soda paste in the other, she found David slumped to the living room floor a few feet away. She plunked the bowl down and cradled his head in her arms.

"David!" she whispered.

He mumbled something and twisted his body to the side. She wiped his flushed face with the wet towel.

Linda heard the commotion and ran in from the back porch.

She stopped abruptly as she caught sight of David stretched out on the living room floor. "What's wrong with him?"

"Go get your father. We've got to get him to a doctor. He must be allergic to bees."

Kurt strode into the room, his face taut. He knelt down and stroked David's head. "Hang in there, Son. We're going to get you to a doctor."

He turned to Jo, lowering his voice. "How are we going to get into town without a car? Damn it! Pike's got the truck. God knows where! And the car won't run. The part hasn't come yet." Kurt couldn't believe the bind that Pike had put them in. He shouldn't have been so cavalier about Pike taking his truck.

"We'll have to wait for Bob to show up. Remember, he was going to go rabbit shooting with David this afternoon?"

Jo arched her head backwards to see Kurt. "He should be here soon. I'm sure he'll loan us his pickup. He'll do anything for David."

She looked down at David's swollen face. His brown eyes were barely recognizable.

"I think this baking soda paste is helping a little. It must feel soothing. He's not groaning now."

~

It was two o'clock before Bob drove down their lane and stopped short of the front porch. Kurt intercepted him before he reached the door.

"David's in bad shape. Got stung by a bunch of bees. We're in a hell of a bind. Mind if I borrow your pickup to drive him into town to see a doctor? Our car needs a part and my truck's gone."

"Gone?"

"Pike took it last night. Hasn't turned up yet."

"That's terrible. We've had some arguments, but I wouldn't

guess that he'd take your truck!"

"Me neither."

Bob thrust his keys into Kurt's hand. "Here you go. It's got some gas in it, too. Where you taking him?"

"The hospital in Cody. The emergency room."

Bob waved him away. "You'd better get going! I'll stay here and watch over things until you get back."

"Thanks, buddy. Shouldn't take too long. The roads are dry."

Kurt drove to Cody in an hour on the gravel road. He and Jo couldn't miss the big "Hospital—Emergency Entrance" sign as they drove up Sheridan Street. The emergency room was empty except for the middle-aged lady at the admittance desk. She peered up at Kurt above the dark gray rim of her glasses that rested midway down her nose.

"Can I help you, sir?"

Kurt glanced down at David leaning on his shoulder, his face still pale. Jo stood on David's other side, forming a protective wedge as they stood before the admittance clerk.

Kurt's voice bore the drumbeat of urgency. "My son needs to see the doctor. He got stung by a swarm of bees earlier today. He passed out at the house. He must be allergic to bees."

"The doctor can see him as soon as I get some basic information. Your name?"

"Glover. Kurt and Jo. Our son here is David."

~

When the doctor finally strode into the room, relief poured over Jo and Kurt. He was young, possibly in his late twenties, with thick black hair like Kurt's. Kurt and Jo tripped over each other explaining how David got into this fix.

"He's a good driver. Knows how to drive that John Deere. You just couldn't see the hive from your tractor, could you, Son?"

David mumbled, "No, Dad. The alfalfa was too tall, but I knew I was getting close."

"Don't worry, folks," the doctor said. "This isn't the first time a kid has come in here with bee stings. But your body didn't take to them, eh young man?"

"No, sir!" David smiled weakly as Kurt grasped his arm.

The doctor gave his appraisal. "Your son is going to be okay. He's allergic to bees, but this shot should do the trick. The swelling will subside in a few hours." After giving David the injection, the doctor sent him home with the family.

~

By Sunday night, there was no sign of Pike or of Kurt's pickup. Jo was convinced they'd never see either one again.

But Kurt held firm. "He'll be back either tonight or tomorrow morning, in time for work."

Jo was furious. "How can you be so naïve, Kurt? He put David's life in jeopardy! And he sure doesn't give a damn that he left you stranded on this ranch."

"I'm as mad as you are about being left high and dry the whole weekend, without a way to take David to the doctor. It's hard to swallow, but Pike's going to show up with the pickup. There's nothing we can do until morning."

~

At breakfast Monday morning, the family still buzzed about the missing hired man.

"You're wrong on this one, Dad," David said.

"No, he isn't," Linda shouted, pointing to the truck coming down the lane. "Here he comes!"

They charged the front door to catch a glimpse of the familiar yellow and black pickup rolling toward the house. When it came to a stop, the door swung open and Pike jumped to the ground.

"Well, if it isn't you," Kurt growled, planting his feet into the packed dirt. "My family was sure we'd never see you or the pickup again."

Pike's eyes bored a hole into the ground. "Yes, sir. Sorry to worry you all. I went into Powell to get a few things and decided to spend the night."

"You mean three nights?"

Pike shifted his blocky body. "Yes, sir. Three nights."

"I don't mind you borrowing my truck for a trip into town so long as you let me know before you leave. But three nights is too long. Turns out, besides losing sleep over it, we needed that pickup on Saturday to get David to the hospital after he rammed the beehive with his tractor."

Kurt's face grew redder, and his whole body shook. He pointed his finger at Pike in anger.

"Those bees were mad as hell. They swarmed his tractor and followed him back to the house. He got stung real bad. We found out he's mighty allergic to bees. My car wasn't running either, so we were in a real fix."

Pike's back stiffened. His voice quivered as he glanced at David. "Oh, my God," Pike said. "You made it into town then?"

"Yes, we did, thanks to Bob. He loaned us his truck."

"You went to Powell?"

"No. Cody. If we'd gone to Powell, we would have found my pickup and taken it off your hands."

Pike was stone-faced. "Sorry to have caused you so much trouble. I never figured on that happening."

"That's the point, Pike. We didn't know David would ram a beehive either. Remember this the next time you decide to spend the weekend at the cat house in Powell 'cause you sure as hell won't have a job when you return."

Pike's face blanched.

"Yes, sir."

He glanced sideways at the whole family staring at him and shuffled towards Jo.

"Sorry ma'am. Don't know what got into me."

"Neither do we, but I hope you heard Kurt. We depend on your word around here."

He tipped his hat toward her. "Yes, ma'am. Understand." He sputtered, and strode toward the barn to begin the day's work.

6

———————

THE FENCE

"When will you pick us up, Daddy?" Jean asked. "After mowing?"

"Don't forget us!" Linda shouted at his back as he leapt across the dry creek bed to his pickup.

He glanced around. "I won't. Now remember, girls. Keep the sheep away from that hole in the fence."

"We will, Daddy." Like cowgirls entering a rodeo arena on horseback, they waved in unison.

He spun a U-turn back to the ranch. Gravel scattered everywhere. The billowing dust cloud thinned gradually to a single horizontal band wafting over the road.

Linda squeezed Jean's small hand. It felt clammy. She wondered how they would keep the sheep from crossing the road if the herd came their direction.

Their house sat high on the far riverbank above the Clarks Fork as it flowed to the Yellowstone. Though two stories high and only two miles away, it looked like a playhouse with the Absarokas towering behind.

Jean wrested her hand free. "What are we going to do now?" She started poking around the dry ditch bed, kicking the chunks of dirt with her faded tennis shoe.

Linda stared at the small pile left behind by her father for their sheep-watching job: an old army blanket, a metal lunch pail filled with roast beef sandwiches and cookies, and a thermos of lemonade. Her mother had made the sandwiches before break-fast while Linda stuffed a sheaf of paper dolls and a bag of marbles into a homemade cotton bag for her and Jean.

She shoved the blanket into Jean's arms. "Here. Take this near the fence. I'll bring the rest."

Jean sidled up the ditch bank toward the fence post that dangled from two loose strands of barbed wire as Linda trudged closely behind with the rest of their gear.

"There's a good place to spread the blanket." Jean pointed out the clumps of bunch grass near the post. Pale green patches bordered the golden field of wind-swept grasses.

Jean tossed the frayed army blanket over the grass. Stomping hard, the girls flattened the blanket over the sticky hillocks. Linda plunked her load down and grabbed some rocks to hold the blanket corners.

"These rocks are too small. One gust of wind and this blanket will be stuck on that barbed wire."

Jean gazed at the small band of sheep lolling across the field. "That's funny. Maybe the blanket will scare the sheep away, like a scarecrow."

"I doubt it. They're too dumb to notice."

Linda stepped off the blanket to check out the post dangling mid-air. The sprung wire still pointed to the sky. When she pushed against the post to see how much spring was left, the top row of barbed wire groaned from the strain. She stopped, afraid another strand could pop loose.

~

The morning seemed to stretch forever. The girls ate the two giant oatmeal cookies from the lunch pail before the sun reached its noontime zenith.

"What can we do now?" Jean asked her older sister.

Linda scooped up some pebbles from the edge of the ditch and slipped them into Jean's hands. "Here you go. Let's see if we can get the sheep's attention." They tossed pebbles in the direction of the sheep grazing across the rocky field, but the sheep were unfazed by the commotion.

"Guess they're not going to charge the fence," Linda said.

Linda dug into the cotton bag. "Look. I brought some of my paper dolls." She handed Jean the Betty Grable doll outfitted in a one-piece bathing suit and kept the Debbie Reynolds doll for herself.

They sat down on the army blanket and started pushing the little white tabs over the dolls' shoulders. A gust of wind came out of nowhere. The cutouts fluttered out of reach before touching down on nearby sagebrush.

Jean dived to salvage their treasures. "Got them!" she squealed. She held a crumpled Betty Grable evening gown in one hand and the Debbie Reynolds doll in the other.

"Look what you've done. They're wrecked."

"Nuh-uh. I can straighten them out. Just watch." She tried to flatten the mashed cutouts on her leg. Debbie Reynolds' neck was broken at an angle, her face flopping against her chest.

"Don't bother." Linda stomped away, determined not to speak to her sister the rest of the day.

~

The heat of the simmering day finally broke the silence. "Why don't we play a game?" Linda said. "Next time we see a car coming, we'll be ready to wave. Maybe they'll stop, and we can ask what time it is."

It seemed like hours before they saw the next dust cloud erupting on the road from Belfry, the nearest town. "A car's coming!" Linda hollered. The girls ran to the edge of the ditch bank along the road, positioning themselves for action. When the gray sedan came close, the girls waved and whistled. Jean held out her red kerchief as if to signal a racecar.

"It's the Kowalski's!" Linda yelled.

The car slowed to a halt. Linda recognized Tom Kowalski. His ranch bordered the road across from their sheep field. As he strode toward them, she forgot to ask him the time.

"What are you girls doing out here on this hot summer day?"

"Daddy wants us to guard the sheep so they don't cross the road and eat your mowed hay. He said green hay can bloat their stomachs," Jean said.

Linda pointed to the broken fence. "Yep. The fence is broken and Dad wants us to guard the sheep until he can fix it. The posts are rotten, so he has to buy new ones. Wanna see?"

"Sure."

The girls led him across the dry ditch to the stretch of fallen fence. They stepped over sagebrush to get a close look.

"Yep. It's in bad shape. Bet your dad hasn't been able to tear himself away from haying to fix it."

"That's right!" they beamed, grateful that he understood.

Mr. Kowalski bent down to pick up something in the grass. "Look here. It's a piece of rusted barbed wire. Must've sprung loose when your father tightened the wire last time. Don't want you girls stepping on it," he said, tossing it into the posthole.

"That's nasty-looking!" Linda said. "Like I said, I'm sure Dad will fix this fence soon."

"No doubt. Tell your dad I'll be glad to help him out. Well, I'll be going. You girls take care now." He straddled the ditch to get to his car.

"Sure will," Linda said. The girls waved as his car dropped out of sight below the river bench.

Something nagged at her. She could hear her father telling their mother weeks ago, "I've got to get that damned fence fixed."

But most of the summer was gone, and the fence was still down. Her father didn't want to use his hired men to do the job, and he didn't like to ask the neighbors for help. He'd wait until the haying season was over and do it himself.

Only a few cars drove by after Tom Kowalski left. Some of them had honked but no one stopped. The girls could tell it was close to noontime by the shortness of their shadows on the ground. Jean's growling stomach was a good sign too.

"I'm hungry."

"Me, too. Let's sit on the blanket and get our lunches out," Linda said.

They stomped again on the bumpy spots until the blanket was flat enough for them to sit down. Before long, they were sharing slurps of lemonade from the thermos bottle and taking bites of their roast beef sandwiches.

~

Linda saw the dust cloud of the oncoming car first. "It's coming from Belfry. We'd better hurry. I don't want to miss this car!" Linda shoved leftover sandwich pieces into the pail and stood up to flag down the car. The car was finally in sight.

They yelled and Jean waved the red kerchief until the car rolled to a stop. A scrawny man about as tall as their father stepped out of the old green car. He wore Levi's and a long-sleeved, plaid shirt with pearl buttons. He took his time coming around his car to the girls' side of the road. He looked their father's age, in his thirties. But his face was weathered and his cheeks caved in, as if he needed a home-cooked meal more than a job.

"Could you tell us the time?" they asked.

The girls stood together on the other side of the dry ditch, in front of the broken fence, several feet away from him. He stood still, closely inspecting them. His sunken cheeks were lined with deep creases. His thin lips looked stuck together by glue. Linda began to feel queasy over his long silence.

"The time? You don't know it's past noon already?" he said at last. He pulled a round watch from his front pocket.

"It's a quarter to one."

He picked up the conversation, shifting to a voice so soft they could barely hear. "How're you girls doing today?"

As the man tugged at the giant, round, silver buckle on his leather belt, Jean sidled up to Linda. He pulled the belt loose, leaving the giant buckle dangling in front, and started to unzip his Levi's. Linda's mouth suddenly felt parched, as if the hot summer sun had baked all the moisture out of her.

"Wanna see?" he asked. His lips barely moved as he folded his right hand over his open Levi's.

Linda shivered. It hit her that he was doing something bad. This man shouldn't be unzipping his pants in front of girls like her and Jean. Beads of sweat fell off the tip of her nose. She gazed away from his hands to his feet. There were cracks in his worn pair of leather cowboy boots. A big dirt clod stuck to one heel.

Maybe he was one of those drifters her mother talked about. She remembered her mother saying drifters were men who didn't have families and came to Wyoming in search of work on the ranches each summer. Her pulse thickened. She grabbed Jean's hand for reassurance.

"Ouch!" Jean squealed.

"Hey, no reason for you girls to be afraid. I can take you home. Where do you live?" he said.

"Go away! We don't like you. Anyway, Daddy wants us to watch the sheep today so we can't go to our house now," Jean said.

"Stop it, Jean!" Jean said too much, as usual. Linda raced through the possibilities. Could they run to the Badura's or the

Kowalski's? The midday heat reflected from the roof of the Our Lady of the Mountain Catholic Church where they sometimes went on Sundays. The church perched on the hill behind the Badura's ranch compound. But it was too far away, and they would have to cross the ditch in front of the man and his car first.

"Why don't you get in?" the man said, motioning toward his car.

The girls didn't budge. The intense summer sun stayed suspended overhead.

"I'll give you a few minutes to think this over," he warned. He pulled up his zipper and stepped slowly toward them.

Linda pushed Jean backwards near the dangling fence post and faced the man directly. "My dad is coming back to get us soon, so you'd better leave." She didn't care if it wasn't exactly the truth. Maybe it would get him to leave.

He shifted his stance as if he was getting ready to cross the ditch bed. She grabbed some rocks and threw them at him. They bounced off his pants into the dirt but he didn't flinch.

"Hey, missy. Stop throwing those rocks, d'ya hear?"

She bent down again to pick up more rocks. Jean joined her this time.

All of a sudden, he froze.

"A car's coming," he muttered. He looked in the direction of a dust cloud erupting near the Frakers' place. He tucked in his shirt and walked to his car. The door slammed shut. The car started and he was gone. The girls watched as the car disappeared below the river bench. He headed to the bridge a quarter mile below the lane to their ranch, in the direction of Cody.

"Why'd you push me so hard?" Jean asked. "You're just a scaredy-cat!"

Linda shook. "You're wrong! He's a bad man! He was going to hurt us."

When his car was out of sight, Linda looked around. What if

he returned? She could see the poplar-lined lane leading to the Badura's house a mile away. Maybe they should run there and ask for help. But they would have to follow the road most of the way. Too far, and he might come back.

"Let's back away from this road. Duck your head and bend down low!" She shoved her sister below the loose strands of barbed wire.

They hurried through grass stubble and cactus inside the field, searching for a low spot where they could hide. The sheep grazing across the field never looked up. She stepped into a swale filled with stalks of tall grass, almost losing her balance.

"Sissy! Over here." They crouched down together.

"What about the car that was coming from Belfry?" Jean asked.

"We'll yell and wave if it's someone we know."

They waited but the car didn't come. They decided he might have taken the road to Powell instead.

"Sissy! Look!" Linda pointed the other direction.

A plume of dust rose above the river bench.

Linda shuddered. "He's coming back!"

They stared at the trail of dust. As the car approached, she yanked Jean to the ground. "It's him. Stay still."

The car sputtered to a stop, spewing gravel.

They huddled together in the bunch grass, feeling the prickly dry stalks of grass poke through their bare arms and legs.

Linda whispered to Jean, "Stay down, Sissy. If he comes this way, we'll run to the river."

Only the sound of fluttering grasshoppers and occasional shuffling of sheep broke the shimmering midday quiet.

"Where is he?" Jean whispered.

"I don't know."

The girls shivered in the hot sun.

"I'm thirsty," Jean said.

"Shhh. Hold on. There he is!"

"What're you doing there?" He hollered down at them.

"You better leave us alone," Linda threatened as she and Jean stood up. She shuddered as he moved towards her. He took two or three leaps over stubble and grabbed her blouse. She screamed. The sleeve ripped.

"Stop it!" Jean pounded his back as fiercely as she could.

The man pulled out his pocketknife and waved it at them. Linda stood still, but Jean kept pounding him in the back until he reached around and shoved her to the ground.

He ordered Linda, "Stay down there with your sister, missy." He pointed to the old army blanket.

Jean saw the dust cloud before he did. "Look! A car's coming!" He glanced up. As quick as a rabbit crossing the road, he shoved his knife into his Levi's and bolted to his car.

The car's engine sputtered.

"What if he can't get it started?" Jean asked.

They waited. The motor clunked each time he turned the ignition. Finally, it caught on. Loose gravel spit from the car's back wheels as he pulled away again.

"He's gone!" Linda whispered. She poked her head above the grass stalks to catch a glimpse of the road. His car dust soon disappeared like a funnel cloud in the afternoon heat.

They swigged some lemonade from the thermos, spread out the army blanket in the swale near the broken fence, and resumed sentry duty for cars coming from either direction.

∾

A yellow and black pickup rumbled their direction.

"It's Daddy!"

They waved frantically to get his attention. When he stopped, they ran to the ditch bank, yelling and crying. Mr. Brown leaped from the truck bed, trailing Kurt across the ditch.

"What's going on here?" Kurt demanded.

"This man stopped his car and unzipped his pants. He wanted to take us to the ranch, but I shouted at him to go away." Jean's words ran into themselves.

"Yes, Daddy." Linda said. "He left because a car was coming but he came back."

"Did he hurt you? Did he hurt you, girls?" His deep voice quavered. He'd never seen his girls so upset. He hadn't dreamed anyone would harm them out here in nowhere. So few cars came through the valley on this dirt road each day.

"No, Daddy, but please take us home with you!" Linda begged him.

"Of course! I was going to Powell to get a part for the combine. Not now." His head jerked backward at the sight of Linda's blouse. "What happened to your blouse?"

Linda looked down at the torn sleeve and choked back sobs.

"The sleeve ripped when he yanked my arm. He pulled out his pocketknife and said to stay down on the blanket."

"Yep, Daddy," Jean said. "I screamed at him and pounded his back but he swung around and shoved me down. Next thing was he ran to his car when he saw that dust cloud."

"Girls!" he said, wrapping his arms around them. "When did he leave here?"

"Right before you got here," Jean exclaimed.

Kurt grimaced. God damn it! How could he have left them alone here?

"You might have passed him, Daddy," Linda's voice faltered.

"Hmm. I waved at a guy in a Studebaker. He passed me by as I came up the bench from the bridge. Jesus Christ! I'll bet it was that guy."

"I-I don't know if it was a Studebaker," Linda stammered. "Anyway, it was old and green."

"It's alright. We'll find him. You girls get in the pickup." The girls slid onto the cab bench while Kurt took Mr. Brown to the top of the ditch, in front of the downed fence.

Linda nudged Jean. "Find him? Did you hear what Dad said?" she whispered.

"Yep," Jean said. "Daddy's really mad!"

The girls watched as Mr. Brown nosed the bunch grass and lay down quietly, not far from where the girls had placed the blanket.

~

Kurt wheeled the truck around and headed back to the ranch. "We're going to look for this man if it takes all day. But first, I'm gonna stop by the house. Get David's help, and see if your mother wants to go." He wasn't sure what he was going to do if he found him, but his shotgun was there to scare the hell out of him, or shoot him if he had to. He blanched at his own anger. He didn't say more, and the girls knew not to ask.

"What does he look like?" he asked at last. His voice was lower than Linda could remember.

"He's almost as tall as you, Daddy," Linda said. "But he's skinnier and has shaggy brown hair."

"He had on a dingy green shirt with pearl buttons and dirty Levi's," Jean added.

Kurt honked twice at Jo working in the garden, and spun to a stop in front of the house. He waved at her to come in as David pulled into the lane on a John Deere tractor. "Hey, Son!"

David drew closer. "Yes, Dad?"

Kurt's mouth was taut, his gray-green eyes narrower than usual. "A man tried to hurt the girls when they were watching the sheep across the river there," he growled.

David was wide-eyed. "*What?*"

"It doesn't bear repeating, Son. I want you and Bob to drive over there. I left Mr. Brown next to the ditch, by the fallen fence. Flag down cars and ask if they've seen this guy. I think I passed him before I reached the field. He was heading for Cody. Linda says he's tall and skinny."

David leaned against the front fender of Kurt's pickup. "What kind of car is he driving?"

"Could be that Studebaker I passed. If not, it's hard to say. The girls were too scared to notice the details."

David tried to lighten up his father. "Not surprising. They're not into cars like me!"

Kurt managed a thin smile. It was true. David knew every make and model of Fords and Chevrolets. Wouldn't be long before he'd be able to get a permit to drive a car on the ranch.

David grew serious again. "Don't worry, Dad. I'll get Bob when he comes in from the field. We can drive his pickup. Where are you going?"

"I'll see if your mother wants to come with me and the girls to search for this guy. Figure we'll head for Cody. When we get to town, we'll stop by the sheriff's office and see if they can help."

Jo heard Kurt as she reached the cab. "What's the matter? What guy are you talking about?"

As Kurt recounted the news, Jo rushed around the truck to reach the girls. She opened the passenger door and stuck her head inside the cab. "Are you girls okay? Did he hurt you?" She stroked their legs and clasped their hands in hers.

"We're okay, Mom. Dad got us before he came back again." Linda whispered.

"This is unbelievable. Never in my life," she sputtered. "Thank God they aren't hurt, Kurt. Remember this morning when I warned you not to leave the girls out there all day?"

Kurt's face reddened. He stared at Jo in disbelief. "Come on! I feel bad enough. Should have gotten that fence fixed sooner,

but you know I never dreamed something like this could happen."

She didn't release her grip of the girls' hands. "Well, the girls
are scared to death. Threatened by some pervert. What's next?"

"I can't say, Jo. But one thing we can do is find this guy. Are
you ready to go?"

She hesitated.

"I don't want to leave you here alone. He might come back!"

"I guess I'd better."

Kurt knew what she was thinking. Jo had never worried about
being alone during the day before. The thought disturbed him.

~

They switched to the Ford sedan and drove all afternoon looking
for the bad man's car. They stopped at every fork in the road and
got out to check for fresh tire tracks. Sometimes it was impossible
to tell fresh tracks from worn ones.

As they came over a ridge closer to Cody, Kurt spotted a
green car—a Ford like his, not a Studebaker. Still, it could be that
guy. He accelerated past the car and flagged him to stop.

"That's not his car, Dad," Linda yelled from the back.

"Shh. It could be him. Or he might have seen the guy on the
road." He motioned to Jo.

"When I get out, slip over here to my seat. If I need to, I'll
signal you to pick me up and we'll head for town."

Jo followed his orders. The two girls sat together like stone
statues in the back.

As Kurt pulled his rifle from the trunk, he noticed the man
had gotten out of his car. Kurt trembled. The man didn't fit the
girls' description. He wore a pair of overalls and leather work
boots. He could have been one of Kurt's neighbors. Kurt shoved
the rifle back into the trunk and quickened his pace past his car

toward the stranger. He caught a glimpse of Jo in the front and his girls in the backseat. They look scared to death. Good thing he put that rifle away. The girls would be traumatized if he had taken a shot. It's blind rage, he admitted to himself. He'd never felt this way before.

Kurt extended his quivering hand. "The name's Kurt. Kurt Glover." His voice trembled. "I've been all over this country looking for a man who threatened my girls today. It's clear you aren't him!"

The man was shook up. "Glad you figured that out! I thought you must have some kind of emergency to flag me down like that." He wanted to know more, but he could tell Kurt was in a hurry.

"You live around here?" Kurt asked.

"Yep. Five miles up the road, on the outskirts of Cody."

"That's where we're headed now. Gonna report to the county sheriff."

"You best get going then."

～

When they reached Cody, Kurt reported the incident to the sheriff.

"No, sir, I'm sorry I can't help you much," he said. "You know how vast this country is. There are so many roads going into the mountains and remote valleys. Places like Sunlight Basin. A guy on the run can disappear real quick."

Stunned, Kurt pressed him hard. "You mean you aren't going to put on a search for him? We've been driving all over this country for hours. We need your help!"

"That's what I'm saying, sir. But we'll send out an alert on the local radio station and on the two-way radios. Officers in every county carry one. Your daughters' descriptions are pretty sketchy, but any law officer in the state can bring this guy in and lock him up if he fits the bill!"

Kurt glared at him. "Seems like more can be done. This man traumatized my girls. Assaulted them in broad daylight."

Jo interjected. "It's frightening to think he's driving around the state right now, probably looking for another victim. Not the same as our rounding up a loose steer on the range."

The sheriff nodded, but stood firm in his convictions. "I understand your reasoning, ma'am. No question he should be locked up. But we're limited in resources. Not enough officers to cover a region this size."

Kurt and Jo shuffled back to the car, their shoulders slumped forward. It was a long trip home. The girls finally fell asleep behind them.

∼

It was close to ten when the family gathered in the living room to hear David and Bob report back. They bragged about how many cars they had stopped along the road.

"You should have seen us, Dad. Bob told me to lie down in the ditch while he stopped the cars. He gave me his rifle in case this guy stopped and was gonna cause trouble. I stayed there the whole time waiting for Bob to give me the signal."

"What were you going to do if you found him, David?" Jo's voice was focused and sharp. "You weren't really going to shoot him if you found him, right?"

"Only if he tried to get away. Like I said, nothing happened Mom. Right, Bob?"

"Yes, Mrs. Glover. No sign of that guy."

Kurt stood up and patted Jo on the shoulder. "It's okay. David knows not to be reckless with a gun. Thank God, nothing bad happened."

~

After the family had exhausted themselves talking, Jo motioned the kids to bed.

"Do we have to, Mom?" Linda asked, her eyes darting to the stairway.

"Can we sleep in your bed tonight?" Jean added.

"I can sleep with you girls in your bed if you want," Jo offered.

As the girls snuggled around their mother, Linda asked, "Can you and daddy promise we won't have to watch the sheep over there ever again?"

"Sure, honey. Never again."

Jo lay wide-awake under the covers until the girls were sound asleep. They're just little girls, she kept thinking. It had never occurred to her and Kurt to warn the girls about men who might try to harm them. They would have to protect the girls better.

~

The next morning, Linda found her father tossing rolls of barbed wire onto the bed of Jimmy.

"Gonna fix the fence today?"

"Yep," he said.

BAD MAN JITTERS

"I'm here, Mom!" she shouted from the front door.

The big house felt empty except for the rattling in the kitchen. Flung across the back of the overstuffed sofa, David's jacket waited to be hung up. The brass floor lamp was lit, waiting for her father to thumb through one of the *Readers Digest*s piled on the oak coffee table.

Linda stood quietly, wondering if her mother had already gone to the bunkhouse. She had promised to meet her there at eleven o'clock sharp to help air out the canvas cots used by the hired men. She glanced at the tall, standing clock in the corner of the room: quarter till eleven. She wasn't late. She heard the rattling again. A muffled sound, on-and-off, came from the kitchen.

She called again from the living room. "Mom, are you here?" Still no answer. Could it be the bad man? Was he doing bad things to her mother?

She tiptoed toward the kitchen door and came to a stop. What if the bad man was in the kitchen, but not her mother? Suddenly, she shook with fear. She could be alone here with the bad man. She leaned on the doorframe and peeked into the kitchen. Nobody there. Only the aluminum pot of beans rattled on the stove. She was overcome with relief, but she felt so foolish. Good thing no one was around to make fun of her.

She spun around and darted out the front door to find her mother. She raced past the row of old cottonwood trees lining the lane, past her mother's summer vegetable garden, straight for the bunkhouse.

She pressed her hip against the screen door to keep it from springing shut as she poked her head inside the room.

"You here, Mom?" she called, peering into the darkness of the unlit room. Toward the back, a narrow band of sunlight from the high, back window formed a white ribbon on the old pine floor

"It's me. Linda!" she yelled into the long bare room.

She recognized the sound of the bristle brush rubbing back and forth across the taut canvas coming from the back. She sighed in relief. There was still time to help her mother. She stepped inside the room, inching along the floorboards as her eyes adjusted to the dim light.

"Hey, girl! What's going on?" a man snarled. He stood alongside a washbowl that the hired men used for shaving and scrubbing their underwear and dirty socks. He held a razor blade next to his chin and swiped his heavy stubble.

She couldn't remember his name, but she knew he was the new hired man. "I'm looking for my mom. I'm supposed to help her air the cots."

"Your mother isn't here," he said, still holding the razor in one hand and a Burma shave brush in the other.

"She said to meet her here."

"I don't know her whereabouts, miss. You best be going." As he took a step toward her, she noticed her sweaty hands. She soft-pedaled backwards across the smooth planks, accelerating as she sensed the light coming through the screen door behind her. When she reached the door, she shoved the warped screen with one hand while peering into the backlit room to locate him. The screen broke loose from the doorframe, propelling her to the ground below the entrance.

"What are you doing?" her mother gasped. "Why were you

in there?" She looked up at the solitary figure in the doorway.

"I was looking for you. You said to meet you here at eleven," Linda gasped.

"Yes. I'm late." She gave her daughter a squeeze, and looked up again at the man.

Linda pointed at him. "It's Daddy's new hired man. He scared me."

"What? Did he try to hurt you?"

Linda shivered, but gave no answer.

The burly, young man stood behind them, holding the razor tight, nicks on his face visible in the sunlight. He jerked slightly at the scene below. He fixed his eyes on Jo, tapping the fingers of his right hand nervously on the doorframe.

Jo recognized him.

"Sparky!" she said. "What happened here? Don't you know Linda? I asked her to help me air out the cots today."

"Yes, ma'am. I do. But I don't know what she was thinking, coming through the bunkhouse like that," he said.

"Looking for me."

Linda glared at him. "Yeah. You scared me when you kept walking toward me with your razor!"

Sparky grimaced, startled by the accusation, "Now, you can't believe I meant you harm, miss. I was just finishing my shave."

Linda didn't budge from her position. She knew he wasn't trying to hurt her, but he made her nervous all over again, like the bad man did. The same cold sweat enveloped her.

Jo looked Sparky in the eye, "Something's not right. Linda is pretty upset. Why are you here shaving in the middle of the day, anyway?"

"I didn't get to it this morning, ma'am, so I figured I'd get a quick shave before getting dinner."

"Well, there's no good reason for you to be inside the bunkhouse midday like this. You should be out helping Kurt in the fields."

"Yes, ma'am." He took a deep breath as if he wasn't getting enough air into his lungs.

"I've got to go inside and fix dinner now. We'll discuss this with you later this evening, after Kurt and I've had a chance to talk."

He jerked around as if he'd been slapped in the face. "Please remember what I said, ma'am. No harm intended to your daughter. I was just freshening up."

Jo grabbed Linda and turned abruptly toward the house, forgetting all about airing the cots.

~

When she told Kurt what happened at the bunkhouse that morning, he peppered her with questions.

"Come on, Jo. Why would Linda come plunging through the door if Sparky hadn't threatened her? We can't be naïve about these things anymore. You know that!"

"He seemed sincere. But then—"

"Damn him!" he started in again. "He should know not to frighten Linda after what she's been through."

"But he doesn't know about that, Kurt."

"Don't matter. He should know better than to approach a young girl in a dark room, razorblade and all."

~

The next morning, Kurt stopped Sparky as he came to the house for breakfast.

"What happened yesterday with my daughter?"

"Nothing, sir," Sparky replied. "She surprised me, that's all."

"You mean you always shave in the middle of the day and

walk around with your razor when you talk to a young girl?" Kurt insisted.

"No, sir. It's a misunderstanding. Like I told the missus, I stopped by the bunkhouse for a quick shave. I wasn't trying to scare your daughter, that's for sure." He extended his right hand to Kurt as a gesture of goodwill.

Kurt didn't reciprocate. "I want you to leave. Get your God-damned things and leave this place now." His hands shook as he spoke.

Sparky stood astonished, but Kurt was firm. The decision was made. By noon, Sparky was gone. Both Kurt and Jo knew that this meant hard times for them all. They were down to three hired men. Not enough men to guarantee twelve-hour days until the haying season ended.

~

The next day, the Kowalskis stopped by the ranch and ended up staying for supper. Everyone was hungry. The pot roast disap-peared in minutes, and the children slipped away to play in the living room.

Jean poked an elbow into Linda's side. "Listen! It's a news bulletin." Linda paused. The Grand Ole Opry had been inter-rupted:

"The Park County Sheriff has received several reports from valley ranch-ers who say they have spotted a man who fits the description of a recent escapee from the Wyoming State Prison. The man has medium brown hair and a few days' growth of beard. He's about six foot, thin, and speaks with a southern drawl. The sheriff has put an all-points bulletin to locate this man and bring him in for questioning."

Linda trembled. Could it be the same man who stopped by the sheep field last month and tried to hurt her and Jean? She gnawed on her fingernails. "Do you think it's the bad man?" she asked Jean.

"Him? Naw. That would be crazy for him to come back here. Especially if he knew that Daddy wanted to kill him 'cause he was so mad."

"Now, Sissy. Dad wasn't *really* going to kill him."

"That's what you think," Jean shot back. "Why else did he take his loaded shotgun when we drove around the country?"

"He wouldn't have used it. Dad won't even go deer hunting with David," Linda replied.

Even so, she wasn't convinced the man wouldn't come back. The girls ran into the kitchen.

"Mom! You won't believe what we heard on the radio," they yelled.

Jo brought Kurt and the Kowalskis in from the back porch to hear the girls retell the story. Everyone offered an opinion on the man's whereabouts until Kurt brought them to their senses.

"We can't afford to be misled by a rootless pervert set loose from state prison in Laramie," he declared. "There are others of his kind, no doubt, but they're not known to travel to this part of the country."

They all nodded in agreement. Everyone felt safer because of Kurt's certainty.

"There's no reason for us to spend more time on this. Let's have some of Irene's good-looking pie."

~

In their bed later that night, Linda absentmindedly rubbed her foot against Jean's. Until yesterday, she hadn't thought about this man for weeks. In spite of what her father said, she felt like he could be in the valley somewhere, six feet tall, scrawny and all.

She winced at the thought of Sparky looking for work again, possibly meeting up with the bad man in his travels. Maybe she had been too nervous in the bunkhouse yesterday. She hadn't imagined her dad would react like that. It was confusing. Maybe she made a mistake. Why didn't she speak up for Sparky? Probably 'cause she was so riled up after being alone with him in that dark room. She hadn't expected him to be there. Surely, he wouldn't come back to teach her a lesson? More likely, he would find another job somewhere else. She felt comforted by that thought.

8

BROTHERLY REVELATIONS

In the soft glow of the early fall afternoon, Linda's new schoolbooks received a good dusting as the school bus rumbled away. She wiped off the dust with her shirtsleeve, careful not to tear the covers.

"Hey, wait for me!" she shouted, but David and Jean were already near the front door.

Her first day of school had been everything she'd hoped for. She hadn't seen either Marcela Gottfried or Lizzie Fraker since May, when school got out. It made her happy to see them again. Marcela looked the same, with her freckled face and arms, and light brown hair trimmed in a bowl cut just below her ears. She was all giggles when she first saw Linda. Lizzie was still tall and skinny, with olive skin and jet-black hair tightly braided halfway down her back. Though Linda didn't look like her two best friends, she was just as giddy with excitement. They danced a jig in the classroom right in front of Miss Lockhart.

The long summer was finally over. All three girls were eager to study together again and help Miss Lockhart with the kids who needed extra help with math or English.

"Hey, Sissy! What are you waiting for?" David yelled.

"I'm coming!" She clutched her books and dashed toward them, but David disappeared inside before she reached the porch. He was saying something to her parents. She couldn't tell what. When he reappeared, he blocked the door.

"Don't go in."

"Why not?" Linda demanded.

"Listen!"

The din of adult conversation wafted through the doorway. Linda leaned against the front window to glimpse inside.

"Who's that with Mom and Dad?" she whispered.

"I don't know," David barked.

"Come on!"

"Okay. He's from Continental Grain."

She'd heard of that company before. She'd seen their name on an envelope that came in the mail. "The folks didn't say anyone was coming today. How'd you know?"

He shrugged. "Ranch business. It's about the lease payment Dad has to make every fall when haying's over."

"But that man hasn't come here before, has he?" She brushed the dust from her shirtsleeve while waiting for his answer.

"Nope. But Dad says we're going through a rough patch. Nothing more."

She pressed her face to the living room window again.

Hunched over the round coffee table, her mother studied the big sheets of paper with columns of numbers. Her father sat stiff as a post in the high-backed armchair, staring at the wall. Once in a while he bent forward, pressed his hands hard onto his knees and nodded. "Yeah. Yeah."

That's what he did when he wasn't really listening, or if he didn't want to hear bad news. It drove her crazy sometimes. She would tell him about something that had happened at school that day: "Daddy, you should have seen how Miss Lockhart screamed at Marvin when she discovered him scrunched like a scared dog behind the door to the library." And he would say, "Oh yeah? Yeah, honey!" It was a sure sign that he wasn't listening to her.

This time was like that. Her father nodded at this man who

had horn-rimmed glasses that squared off his face, and a brand new barbershop haircut that left only a stubble of dishwater brown hair on his head. He didn't seem as tall as her father. Maybe that was because he was sitting down and his gray wool slacks were stretched thin at the seams to hold in his fat.

"I'm going in," she insisted.

"No. Wait!"

She swept past him into the living room. Her mother eyed her sideways, startled. "You kids need to stay outside. Your father and I are talking business with this gentleman. We'll be done soon." As she spoke, Jo grazed the stack of paper on the coffee table with her right arm. She watched helplessly as papers fluttered everywhere.

"Look at what I've done!" She groaned as she reached down to pick them up. "Okay, now. Take your books to your room." Her voice tightened. "Don't dump them on this table."

"I was going to take them to the kitchen. I'm starving!"

Kurt interrupted them. "Your mother has started dinner. Now, scoot. We have business to do."

～

Linda slid past them to raid the fridge. Anything would do. She finished off a small bowl of leftover cottage cheese. It was getting late, almost six thirty. They always sat down to supper at six, even in the fall after the hired men had left.

"When do you suppose they'll be done?" Jean asked.

"Soon, I hope, 'cause I'm getting hungry," David replied.

They heard their father's voice grow louder in the other room.

"He sounds mad!" David said.

"Shh. Listen!"

"No, we can't do that, Mr. Stevens. Absolutely, no way,"

Kurt said. "When I signed this God-damned lease in Seattle three years ago, I told your attorney we were short of cash. I can't make money out of trees. Too few of them anyway in this godforsaken country."

"Mr. Stevens, your company won't find anybody who works as hard as us to make a living off this ranch," Jo said, her voice quivering.

"What's wrong with Mommy and Daddy?" Jean asked.

Linda hushed her. "Now, don't you worry, Sissy. That man will leave soon."

"Why's he being mean to them?"

"He's just a businessman. That's all."

"Yep," David said. "If he demands payment tonight, he'd better realize the closest bank is in Powell."

"We can have Nasty peck on his hand. That'll show him who's boss around here," Linda added. They all laughed in relief.

Jo flung the door open. "You kids get some supper for yourselves. Dad and I will be there in a few minutes."

~

By the time their parents joined them, the roast beef was cold, and the coleslaw was room temperature. It was past seven.

"We're a little later than usual, aren't we?" Kurt plunked down next to David at one end of the table. "I'll have some of that roast beef, honey. I've been smelling it for hours." He tried hard to look relaxed.

"Here you go. Sorry, it's all dried out," Jo added, her voice flat.

Kurt patted her shoulder, but she looked away. He could tell she was upset. Understandable. But he was still digesting what took place minutes ago in the living room. Stevens wouldn't give an inch on the late payment. It drove Kurt mad to think he wouldn't agree to a delayed payment until next fall, after a better harvest put some cash in their pockets again. He just needed a break. One good break and his dream would stay alive! He looked down at the slices of roast beef on his plate. Time to eat.

Linda wondered if Mr. Stevens struck a different deal for the lease payment, a deal which meant they couldn't stay on the ranch until spring. One thing for sure—her parents weren't going to share this with her or Jean. And if they told David, he'd be sworn to secrecy. She couldn't count on any more revelations from him.

She felt locked inside a gray zone, not knowing whether she would live in the same house, or go to Clark school again this fall. She hadn't heard her parents talk about any plans for moving or anything. Would they go back to her grandparents' ranch in Oregon? That was a long way from here.

Linda groaned at her predicament. Why was she left out of these important family decisions? She was as isolated as the hired men.

～

Her mother had stopped making canvas dams for the irrigation ditches on her Singer sewing machine, now making school clothes for Linda and Jean instead. Jean had quit pestering her about what they were going to do after the evening dishes were done. She was in fifth grade now and that meant lots more homework. On weekends, David slept in because he didn't have to join his father and the hired men in the fields all day.

But this year felt different. Although her father's face was once again two shades darker from working long hours every day in the burning summer sun, his forehead etched with worry when he talked with Jo about the size of this year's hay crop.

"I don't know, honey. We're going to have to buy feed for the cattle this year. Not enough hay or silage to last the winter."

Her mother's cheeks looked hollow and her face pinched. "Maybe we can get credit from the Grange until next season?"

He shook his head. "Maybe. Yeah. Maybe."

Even Jean seemed different lately. Not just that she was suddenly taller. She was almost as tall as Linda when they stood back-to-back. Or that she had refused to wear an old pair of Linda's shoes until her parents could get her a bigger size on their next trip to town. No, it was something else that made Linda take a second look at her little sis.

On a trip into Powell the week before, Jean asked her mother to stop at the library so she could check out some Nancy Drew mysteries. This was a first for Jean. She hadn't shown much interest in books before. She would say, "I don't want to sit in the house reading a book. I wanna play outside." She liked playing fetch with Mr. Brown or tossing horseshoes. Maybe she'd like school this year, too.

School always started the day after Labor Day, the same time of year when her parents celebrated their anniversary. This year, September 2nd fell on a Sunday, giving her father time to join her, David and Jean in a game of Monopoly. Their mother made an angel food cake as they played. The cake took a dozen eggs, though she used only the whites.

Linda and Jean dreaded having to gather that many eggs from those hens. When they reached into the nests high above their heads to get the eggs, they had to dodge cackling hens flying from their high perches, their loose feathers causing a dust storm inside the chicken house.

~

After weeks of working long days and pouring over bills with Jo at night, her father seemed like his old self again. Maybe that meeting with the grain company man went better than she had thought. Linda steered clear of bringing up the subject of the ranch business with David.

Her parents must have figured out a way to make the payment, after all. Like the quiet after a summer thunderstorm, life on the ranch returned to normal. She and Jean were back to gathering eggs after school, and David became an after-school ranch hand again.

Her mother spent most of September restocking the basement shelves with quarts of applesauce made with apples from their orchard, canned green beans, shucked corn, and other vegetables from their garden. Many afternoons, she would place seven quart-sized Mason jars filled with homemade applesauce into a giant canning kettle on the kitchen stove and boil them for 25 minutes. It must have comforted her to know that the basement shelves were filling up again with her new supply of Mason jars. Jo was preparing for the long cold winter ahead. In a few weeks, they would all be hunkering down, just like the cattle and the sheep.

9

TIME OF RECKONING

The sliver of light cast an eerie glow into the darkened kitchen. Linda's bare feet stumbled on the cast iron stove as she reached for the stairwell door next to her parents' bedroom. She was annoyed with herself. After all, she had learned how to come downstairs quietly to go to the bathroom at night without disturbing them. Luckily, her parents were deep in conversation, propped up by pillows in their double bed. She lingered a little longer before going back upstairs. It was a good chance to hear things they wouldn't share with the kids.

"But, Kurt. There's plenty of hay from this year's crop."

"Looks that way, but it won't last long. This crop was the worst we've had. The late spring shortened our growing season. And remember how the August rains damaged the hay rows before we could bale?" His hopes for a good harvest had been dashed. It meant another long winter with few reserves.

She nodded absently. Kurt was right. Every time they got their hopes up, they were shot down by bad weather and wild storms that attacked with a vengeance. They couldn't count on things going their way, and spring seemed so far away.

"My guess is we'll need to buy some hay on the market by mid-winter and we're going to pay a hefty price for it. The steers didn't bring enough this year either."

A few weeks ago, he and David had taken two truckloads of steers to market in Billings. "We should have gotten a better price. There's a glut on the market this year. Mild winters will do it."

"Mild?"

"Yes. The old-timers say so. They remember years when Northerners ripped through these mountains and caught their cattle before they could bring them in from the range. Guess we're lucky in that way." He fixed his gaze on their old dresser across the room.

"I think we should wait until spring to decide about renewing the lease," she said.

"We don't have that option. They can end the lease early on us. We're late with this year's payment. I told Stevens we'd catch up by the end of the month. That'll eat up a chunk of our cash from our sale of the cattle last week."

She gasped. "You really think they would do that to us?"

"Yep. They figure they have the right. It's just a business to them. It's not about family, that's for damned sure."

"That's awful." She stuffed the thin pillow behind her back again. "Maybe we should explain the whole situation and ask for more time." She looked up at Kurt in her most hopeful way.

"You mean about how we don't have enough cash to get through the winter? You heard him yourself. That won't work."

"No. I mean we should tell him about *my* situation."

"What situation?"

"I'm pregnant."

"You are?" He sputtered in disbelief.

She smiled. "Don't act so surprised. You know the rhythm method is about as effective as taking an aspirin. I haven't had a period in three months."

He chuckled softly. "No kidding! We're going to have a baby?"

"By my count, it'll arrive during lambing season. I'll be just like one of those swayback ewes!"

He laughed. "With twins?"

"Heavens no! What a thought." She shuddered beside him, a diminutive figure in her red chiffon nightgown.

"Why didn't you say something?" he asked.

"I knew you had a lot on your mind. And another child..."

"Come on, Jo. It'll be fine." He threaded his fingers through her hair. "Your hair has gotten long, hasn't it?"

"I guess so. I hardly have time to notice it."

He stroked her hair again. "Not me. I always think it's beautiful." She succumbed to his charm, softly pressing her head against his shoulder.

It was obvious her parents had no time for a prowling kid making her way back upstairs after using the downstairs bathroom. Linda withdrew into the stairwell, outside the sweet silence of her parents' room, and crept upstairs to relay the news. She could hardly wait to tell David and Jean. They wouldn't believe her. No matter that she might have to wake them up to tell them.

She rushed into her and Jean's bedroom first, reached across the bed and shook her sister's shoulder. "Guess what, Sissy?"

Jean rolled over and scrunched up her face. "What?"

"Mommy's going to have a baby."

That got Jean's attention. "Really? Why are you saying that?"

"'Cause it's true. I heard Mom and Dad talking when I was downstairs."

Jean wriggled free of the bed covers to reach the pine floor with her bare feet. "Let's go tell David!"

They scrambled across the hallway.

"What's going on?" He bolted upright in his bed.

"Nothin' much. We have some news you might be interested in though." Linda savored the suspense.

"Yeh?"

Jean couldn't stand it. "Mommy's going to have a baby!"

"What?!"

"Yep. I heard them say so," Linda said.

David turned red, embarrassed as could be. "Did they say when it's supposed to be born?"

"Mom said this winter, during lambing season. I wonder how Dad will get her to the hospital if there's a blizzard."

"He'll figure it out. Dad always knows how to get to town if he needs to. He's not afraid of icy roads or deep snowdrifts."

They pledged to keep the news a secret and wait for their parents to fess up. Their mother's belly was bound to get bigger. Armed with a plan, they marched single file down the narrow staircase to the warmth of the kitchen.

⁓

On a brisk October morning, when the sky formed an endless swath of blue, Kurt left the ranch for a meeting in Billings.

"Ranch business, kids. I'll be back by supper," he announced at breakfast. "David, you take care of things. See if you can fix that rear tire on the tractor. It's low on air. Girls, help your mother today."

"Yes, Dad," David affirmed for the trio before splitting outside ahead of his father.

"Good luck, honey," Jo said. Her soft voice trailed him as the screen door banged shut behind the children.

After lunch, Jo walked down the lane a quarter mile to the main road to get the mail. A *Farm & Seed* catalog and a letter postmarked September 19th from Palm Desert, California were mixed in with the pile of bills. Jo recognized her aunt's handwriting on the envelope and quickened her pace to get back to the house. It was curious that Ava would write again. Too early for a Christmas card.

Linda watched her mother drop the mail on the kitchen table. "A lot of mail today, huh Mom?"

"More than usual." She tore Ava's letter open. "Oh, my!"

Linda stopped drying the lunch dishes. Her mother sat stock-still, gripping the letter in her hands.

"It's from Aunt Ava. I haven't heard from her in months."

"Something wrong?"

"Let me finish."

Linda shuffled behind her mother to read the letter. Blunt handwriting in dark blue ink filled the page.

"Dearest Jo and Kurt, We have terrible news. Our darling Francy died last month in a fall in the San Bernardino Mountains. She was hiking with her Girl Scout troop. She ran ahead, eager to reach the summit first. They didn't have time to warn her about the cliff. They said she must have lost her footing on loose dirt. She fell a couple hundred feet."

Before Linda could finish reading it, her mother folded the letter along the creases and slid it back into the envelope. Linda stood quietly behind her for a minute, hoping they could talk about this shocking news. But Jo crossed the room and tucked the letter inside a kitchen drawer crowded with bills and other important papers. Linda could tell her mother didn't want to discuss it.

～

Francy dead? Couldn't be! When she came here last summer, though she was barely thirteen, she looked like someone on the cover of Seventeen magazine. Her brown hair was styled in a pageboy, and she wore make-up and lipstick almost as red as her mother's. She sure didn't have the look of a Wyoming ranch girl ready for outdoor adventures, but it turned out she was coura-geous and brave.

That rafting adventure showed Francy had guts. Though she'd only swum in a backyard pool before coming to the ranch, she agreed to go on David's homemade raft through the rapids of the Clarks Fork. That was more risk than Linda was willing to take. Swimming in quiet pools along the river's edge was risky enough for her.

Yet things went haywire that day. Linda could still hear Francy's screams when she was flung like a rag doll into the rapids when their raft rammed a boulder. Linda and Jean helped drag her to shore after her foot got snagged under water in the fast current.

Linda remembered, too, when she'd showed off her collection of eight-by-ten glossy photos of movie stars posted with thumb-tacks to the wall above her bed, Francy claimed to have met some of them during visits to movie studios like MGM and 20th Century Fox in Hollywood.

"If you come see us, we can go there. They'll give you a stack of pictures, signed by famous stars like Lana Turner and Loretta Young."

That whetted Linda's appetite. After Francy left the ranch with her parents, swollen ankle and all, Linda had dreams of visiting her in California, maybe after school got out next year.

She knew it wouldn't happen now. How could things change so fast? Francy was so ornery at times, sassing back at her parents, yet funny and adventurous, too. Now she's dead?

～

Linda caught up with her mother later that afternoon. "You really love Ava, don't you Mom?"

"Well, yes, honey. I-I do," she stammered. "She's always been my favorite auntie. When I was a young girl, she would invite me to make cookies with her, and pick currants near the creek where they lived in southern Oregon. She helped take care of me and my sisters and brothers after our mother left us to live with another man. That was before she adopted children of her own,

Francy and Sarah."

Linda was stunned. She'd never heard this story about her mother's childhood before. No wonder her mother was so happy when Ava and Charlie traveled all the way from California to stay with them.

~

Just as he'd promised, her father arrived home before dark. "Good to be home," he said as he strode into the kitchen, but he seemed more subdued than usual.

"Honey, can I see you for a minute before dinner?" He motioned to Jo. They stepped into the back porch to talk. When they returned, Jo held her apron like a dishrag. Her face looked ashen.

Kurt started the conversation with a bang. "Kids, we're going to leave the ranch. Time to move on."

"Mr. Stevens didn't come through for us?" David blurted.

"No, Son. He wants his money now, and we just don't have it. But there's a house in Badger that'll hold us all."

"Badger?" David asked. The girls were all ears.

"Badger Basin. You know, where the gas flare is."

"Are there real houses there besides the Weber's?" Linda asked.

"'Course there are, honey," he answered confidently.

Jo joined him in solidarity. "You've seen those Quonsets before, I'm sure."

Kurt nodded. "Yep. They're not much to look at, but they're well insulated. They look bad because no one has lived in them since the gas company abandoned the place in the forties. They were company housing for the workers."

Jo fell silent. She and Kurt didn't have many options once they lost their lease. Kurt had looked into the possibility of working for the Frakers on a year-round basis so they could stay in the

Clark valley, but Mickey said he couldn't afford it. They considered moving to the nearest big city, Billings, but only Jo had the skill set to get an office job. That left Badger as their best bet for now. They could rent one of the Quonset houses for a hundred dollars a month, and only have to pay for electricity, and the kids could still go to Clark School.

That was Linda's first question. "Can we still go to school at Clark?"

Kurt was emphatic. "You sure can."

"That's good, Dad!" David and Jean grinned too.

~

Linda's good mood quickly dissolved when she began to think about Badger Basin. Such a desolate place. Besides the remnants of the gas drilling operations and the Quonset houses, there was nothing but sagebrush and dirt as far as you could see.

David seemed to have the same reaction. "Isn't there a better place for us to go?" he pleaded. "Maybe we could rent a house in Powell or Cody."

"No, Son. Your mother and I have thought about this. We've checked into some options. Critical thing is to get into a house we can afford before your mother gets too big, and live close by so I can work some part-time jobs on the ranches this winter."

The kids had never seen their father look so dejected. His easy smile and happy laugh had dissipated to a stern shadow of gloom.

Linda finally spoke up about the news in Ava's letter. "Daddy, do you remember cousin Francy? Mom got a letter about her today from Aunt Ava."

"That's right," Jo said, her eyes downcast. "A terrible thing. Francy fell off a cliff in the San Bernardino Mountains near their home." A lone tear slid down her cheek. "She was hiking with her Girl Scout troop and ran too far ahead for them to warn her about the cliff. They found her crumpled body later, far below the bluff."

Kurt blanched. "Oh, my God!"

"Ava and Charlie are terribly shaken. It's an unbelievable loss for them. Leaves a huge hole since Sarah left home in '55 to get married."

"Hmmm." He stabbed a piece of pot roast on his plate. His slender body needed some nourishment, but his appetite was gone. "Horrible thing. Tragic." He shook his head as he slid some meat onto his plate.

The table was as quiet as Linda could remember for a family meal. There wasn't much more anyone could say. Her father was tired, and her mother looked pale and distraught. They passed the dishes around the table and ate until the food was gone.

At last, she got up from the table and poked a finger in David's side. "Let's go outside. It's too hot in here."

"Yeah. Way too hot," he said.

～

Later, she realized she'd forgotten to ask her father when they would move. She'd find out soon enough. Whenever it was, she and David would have to help out. Jean, too. It was going to be a big job, and they needed to protect their mother from heavy hauling these days.

II

BADGER BASIN, WYOMING 1956

10

TWO FRONT DOORS

"Hey, Dad! Which door should we use?" Linda shouted from the bed of the pickup, her long hair blowing sideways across her face. She leaned forward to survey the entrance to their new home.

"The one on your left."

The Quonset house had two front doors a few feet apart, one to the living room, the other to the kitchen. Sun-bleached and weathered, with peeling white paint, each door had a step-up concrete pad sitting on top hardpan that sprawled for miles around. Nearby, a rusted pipe thrust ten feet out of the ground. Day and night, its gas flare lit the desolate landscape surrounding the abandoned oil and gas field known as Badger Basin.

A tall cottonwood stood in solitude in the Weber's front yard, a short distance from their house. The tree provided the only shade in the former company-owned housing compound. A few scattered buildings had withstood the torments of bitter winters and violent windstorms. They were a reminder of decades past when over twenty oil and gas wells had been drilled deep below the ground.

David signaled his father to a stop as the pickup drew near the doorway to the living room. "Whoa, Dad! Close enough!"

The faded green couch, piled high with boxes, extended beyond the tailgate. A thick rope crisscrossing a canvas tarp held everything in place.

Linda ran ahead, scouring the bare rooms in search of a place for the furniture. The rooms were smaller than she was used to, but at least there were three bedrooms and a bathroom with a ceramic tub. Cream-colored linoleum speckled with yellow and orange spots covered the floors in every room. Edges flared up in areas along the wall where the glue had dried up.

Kurt and David grunted as they hefted the couch into the front room.

"Where to?" Kurt said.

"Over here. Mom will like it against this wall." Linda pointed to the center of the back wall.

"Okay, honey. Wherever you say!" He and David exchanged smiles at taking directions from her.

Jean had stayed behind with her mother to finish the packing. Linda was glad for that. Her mother had seemed quieter than usual. She was almost four months along, and couldn't fit into most of her clothes anymore. She had complained about not having much energy, and threw up after eating almost every night. It was probably a good thing she didn't have to feed those hired men anymore. Maybe the move to a house without a ranch would be easier on her.

~

Before long, they had unloaded the whole truck. David tossed the rope and tarp onto the truck bed and jumped into the cab alongside Kurt and Linda.

She counted six or seven hauls from the ranch that day. It was only five miles away, but it seemed farther. They'd driven past Badger Basin many times on their way into Powell for groceries, or to have a tooth pulled, but she had never imagined the family might move there.

Her father had put on a brave face about the move. "We're

lucky to find a place to rent before winter sets in," he had said recently. "Most of those old houses aren't fit to live in. The Quonset house is funny-looking with that round corrugated steel roof, but it's big enough for us." He was right.

Kurt was the eternal optimist and Jo, the worrier. That's why Linda liked her father's explanations better than her mother's. He always found a way to make her laugh. Now was a good time for that. She looked for things that would make her feel better about this move. He had promised her that they would still go to Clark School. The school bus would stop at Badger Basin to pick them up, along with the two Weber kids.

And she looked forward to the annual community Christmas party at the lower grade school house in December. She might be asked to play the piano again. The thought took her far away from the move to Badger Basin.

∼

The family grew used to watching tumbleweeds bounce by the kitchen and living room windows, buffeted by the incessant winds that blew across the plains. Their new house sat in the middle of the basin where sagebrush, cactus, and yucca were all you could see for miles around. At night, the tall gas flare provided plenty of light for children to play games outdoors within a quarter mile radius.

Although their ranch was only a few miles down the road from Badger Basin, it felt far away. Kurt became a ranch hand for the Frakers. He was no longer a rancher in charge of hundreds of acres of alfalfa fields, two hundred head of cattle, and a small herd of sheep that grazed the rocky land across the river. Jo's world was smaller, too. She was now in charge of a one-story house with a steel corrugated roof and a cellar below. She didn't have her vegetable garden or apple orchard. And she couldn't step outside the back porch to watch the Clarks Fork flow by when she wanted a break from household chores.

But the school bus stopped early every morning and dropped them off in the afternoon, just like Kurt had promised. It was a longer ride now, but Linda still got to play "Red Rover, Red Rover" during recess and see her friends, Marcela Gottfried and Edna Kowalski, in class every day.

~

In early October, David talked Jo into letting him go deer hunting with Bob Marney in the hills behind the Fraker's place. He felt lucky to be with Bob again. They had become close friends while working together on the ranch during the summers.

"But you need a hunting license," she said.

"Nobody's going to report us," David replied. "Ranchers poach deer all the time around here." It was the ranchers' way of getting even with the deer that foraged their alfalfa crops during the haying season.

"Alright, David. Don't do anything silly now. Stick close to Bob."

David grinned. "Sure thing, Mom."

~

It was Indian summer, with cold nights that left heavy dew on the ground in the morning and days that sometimes warmed up to seventy.

Early the next morning, the two boys got up at four o'clock and loaded their rifles into Bob's '54 Jimmy pickup and set off for the nearby hills.

"We're going to get a forked horn this time," David said.

"You think so? We'll be lucky to find one!"

David grimaced. Bob was probably right. He was three years older and an experienced hunter. He had shown David the draws where the deer lay during the day, moving to graze the alfalfa fields at sunrise or sunset. He also taught him to walk into the wind so the deer wouldn't pick up their scent and run away.

An amazing marksman, Bob carried his Winchester model 70, caliber 308. It was a bolt-action rifle, different from the small twenty-two with tube-pump action that David used to hunt rabbits.

When they got to the base of the hills, Bob pulled up next to a fence and shut off the motor. It was getting towards dawn, barely light enough to pick their way through occasional rocky outcrops, clumps of old sagebrush, and bunch grass to the first draw.

When the morning light grew brighter, they settled into some bunch grass to spot deer. They heard a coyote but never located it. An hour went by before they found their first deer.

"Got it in my line of sight," David whispered while holding his twenty-two steady on his right shoulder. When the shot rang out, the kickback from the rifle stung his shoulder hard. He waited to see if he needed to fire again, but the deer collapsed to the ground.

Bob and David hiked back to the fallen deer.

"Looks like you've got your forked horn," Bob declared. "I didn't think your twenty-two could do it. You've got a good eye. Let's gut him here before hauling him back to the house."

David shrugged his shoulders. "Guess so." He'd forgotten this was the next step. "Sure is a lot more work than rabbits. I just left them in the field for the coyotes."

Bob smirked. "Yeah. Big difference."

Exhausted by the time they dragged the carcass onto the bed of Bob's pickup, they headed home, leaving the offal in the prairie for the coyotes.

~

David ran ahead of Bob into the house. "Mom, I got my first forked horn!"

Jo and the girls came outdoors to have a look.

"Where are you going to put that thing?" Linda asked. She shuddered at the messy sight.

"Can we hang it in the cellar, Mom?"

"I guess so. Be sure to remove all the bullets before you take that rifle into the house."

"I'll do it now so you won't worry." David pulled his rifle to his side and pumped the bullets out of the chamber one by one. He coupled the bullets in his hand as proof for his mother. "Got 'em!" Jo patted his arm in approval.

~

After Bob left, David carried his rifle through the kitchen to his bedroom. Jo stepped back to get out of his way.

"You in a hurry?"

"Naw. Gotta put my rifle away."

Jo returned to fixing dinner. Minutes later, a shot rang out from David's bedroom. Linda screamed from the living room and ran to find her mother.

"What was that?"

Jo stood stock still in front of David's bedroom.

"Mama! Aren't you going in?"

Jo leaned into the door, listening for a sound. Utter silence. She flung the door open, fearing the worst.

"David!" In the semi-dark room, Jo could barely make out David's solitary figure standing alongside his dresser. His hand shook as he pointed to a hole in the top drawer.

"Bore a hole right through it."

Jo rushed forward and pulled David as close as she could to her growing belly. "You're okay. Thank God, you're okay!" Her voice quivered; her pregnant body trembled.

"Sorry, Mom. Didn't mean to scare you." He wriggled free from her grip. "Looks like the only damage is to my old dresser. I knew the gun was empty so I took aim at the dresser, kinda like a practice shot. Didn't expect the rifle to go off, that's for sure."

Linda decided hunting deer wasn't for her. The whole idea of taking a rifle into the prairie before dawn to look for deer while keeping coyotes at bay was enough to convince her to stick with reading books and chasing the boys around the schoolyard during recess.

11

CHRISTMAS PARTY AT CLARK SCHOOL

The gate to the chain link fence was roped back for the annual Christmas party, offering plenty of room for the pickups and cars to pull off the icy road into the dark schoolyard for the big event. Snow fell all day, leaving a thin crust on the frozen ground outside. It was a Northerner, a storm coming from Canada, known for bringing tiny snowflakes, sharp gusts of wind, and temperatures hovering below zero with the wind chill.

Golden shafts of light from the tall classroom windows of the lower grade school house formed irregular rectangles onto the frozen landscape outside, inviting the bundled-up children and their parents in.

Linda had arrived early with her family so she could practice playing the piano. Her Christmas carols greeted arriving partygoers, ringing through the walls to break the crystalline silence of the cold night air.

In the foyer, partygoers hung their heavy wool coats on hooks that lined the west wall. Ranchers greeted each other as they removed their cowboy hats, white from the dusting of snow, and children flung their damp coats on the long bench below the wall hooks.

Men stayed in the foyer sneaking flasks of whiskey from inside their upper coat pockets to share a nip with their neighbors. The wives took potluck dishes, desserts, and their children into the classroom for the party. The room soon buzzed with hearty laughter as the ranchers exchanged stories about getting tractors stuck in mud, fixing broken fences, and how they kept the livestock fed in the dead of winter.

In the classroom, Jo's pregnant belly stretched the front of her bright red tent dress as she helped the women arrange potluck dishes and platefuls of Christmas cookies on the folding tables covered with white tablecloths.

Almost eight months along, Jo felt her face flush from the warmth of the crowded room. Linda watched her mother walk toward the Christmas tree standing in the corner of the room. She flung a fallen string of popcorn to some tree branches above. The scruffy pine, laden with strings of popcorn and multi-colored lights, added glitz to the occasion.

When the buffet was laid out, the children formed lines on either side of the tables. Once seated, the men moved in from the foyer and joined the wives and other adults in heaping their plates with slices of roast beef, scoops of scalloped potatoes, and other side dishes.

Afterwards, Miss Lockhart, the upper grades teacher, led the children in singing Christmas carols. The entire community sang the traditional last song, "Silent Night," as Linda accompanied them on the piano. Their soft voices reflected her peaceful feeling.

The crowd resumed their chatter and the women cleaned up the dishes. Linda saw her father under the doorframe of the foyer, his head tilted down to look Mickey Olmsted in the eyes. Tom Kowalski stood alongside them, his head thrust forward to grasp the conversation.

Tom was one of her father's favorite neighbors. He was a stocky, barrel-chested man. Though his thick Polish accent made him difficult to understand, her father didn't seem to mind. Their conversations were usually short and mixed with a lot of friendly backslapping.

Mickey was on the school board and drove the school bus around the valley each day to pick up the elementary school children. He was a small, wiry man, known for picking fights. Linda could tell her father didn't think much of him. He had told Linda once that he saw Mickey as loud but harmless.

As their argument wafted through the room, Linda got up from the piano bench and edged closer to hear their conversation.

"I saw you as a man who would've taken his family back home to the ranch in Oregon. Not the kind of guy who'd move his family into a Quonset hut out there in that hell hole."

"You know damned well why we moved to Badger Basin." Kurt spoke evenly, with only a hint of emotion, his arms stiff by his side.

"Sure do, Kurt. You never learned how to make a living off your land. If you had, you wouldn't be working as a ranch hand at Fraker's place over the winter."

Her father's voice rang out in the noisy room. "Look, Mickey. What the hell do you know? You're nothing but a bus driver."

Hearing Kurt's charged voice, Jo rushed across the room. She grabbed Kurt's right arm and nosed into the circle. "What's the matter, honey?" Her right arm laid on top her bulging belly, as if protecting the baby growing inside.

Kurt nudged her back. "Mickey's being difficult."

He looked again at Mickey. "I've worked cattle my whole life and these conditions spell trouble for us all. Price of beef has tanked. This hardpan won't grow a decent crop, and thunderstorms cause flash floods that destroy irrigation ditches and wipe out half the crops."

A small crowd formed around the men. Her mother was just behind Kurt, leaning close to Irene, whispering something. Someone tapped Linda on the shoulder.

"Linda, come back! We need you to play the piano." It was her friend Margaret.

"Not now, Maggie!" She tried to shrug her off.

Maggie tugged again at her sleeve. "Please?"

"Okay. One more song." She strode across the crowded, creaky wood floor to the piano bench. As she sat down, she gasped as she saw her father brace his hands against Mickey's chest and shove him backwards. Mickey stumbled to the floor and started cursing him.

"Why you son-of-a-bitch! Guess you don't like me calling you a ranch hand!"

Kurt hung over him, his eyes blazing. Tom stepped between the two, pointing his finger at Mickey, "Sober up, Mickey. We're here for a Christmas party, not a fight."

Mickey reached for a chair to steady himself before wobbling toward Tom. "You stay out of this, you Polack! You're as big a loser as Kurt!"

Tom's face flushed with anger. He muttered something to her father and stepped toward Mickey who retreated backwards to the row of front windows. A couple of the windows had been opened at the bottom to bring some cold night air to the stuffy room.

Tom shouted, "Where do you think you're going?"

Linda sat transfixed. Tom cocked his right arm back and took a full swing at Mickey, smacking his left cheek full-bore. Mickey's backside crashed through the center windowpane. His cowboy boots were the last to glide over the low windowsill as shards of glass flew in all directions.

He landed with a thud on the frozen yard below. Seconds later, Mickey reappeared outside the broken window, his dazed eyes peering into the room as he tried to wipe his bloodied face clean of the snow and grit.

He shouted through the shattered glass to his wife, "Amanda, quick. Get my coat and keys!" She called their two young sons, grabbed her belongings, and ran outside to help her husband.

~

Linda started pounding the piano keys again while her mother worked to calm her father and Tom. Some children joined Linda around the piano to sing more Christmas tunes, but it was too late.

The party spirit had dissolved with the fistfight. The icy air flooded into the room through the jagged glass of the damaged windowpane, displacing warmth with cold, and rustling the Christmas lights on the tree.

The crowd dwindled fast. Parents and their kids yanked coats from the pile in the foyer. Mothers rushed to find their dishes and serving pieces before hustling their children outside. It was time to go home.

12

FROZEN PIPES AND SPRING THAW

On a bitter cold day in early February, Kurt returned from the hospital in Powell to announce the birth of their new baby brother. He beamed at the small crowd gathered around him in Margie Weber's living room—Margie and her daughter Rayla, and his three kids.

"He weighs over eight pounds, and he has a thatch of dark brown hair."

The children squealed in delight.

"Wonderful, Kurt. How's Jo doing?" Margie asked.

"Pretty good. Pretty good." He nodded his head reassuringly. When he turned his back to continue his conversation with Margie in private, Linda strained to hear him.

"She needs to recover from the surgery," he muttered. "Expect I can bring her and the baby home in a few days."

Linda's heart stopped. Her mother hadn't said anything about having surgery to deliver the baby.

"Is she going to be okay?" she asked as evenly as she could. Whatever happened in the hospital, it wasn't likely her father would reveal much.

"Of course, honey. In a few days, she'll be back to her old self."

Linda shrugged, skeptical of his response. "That's good."

"What's his name, Dad?" David asked.

"Christopher. How's that sound? Your mother's choice."

He smiled. "I like it!"

～

Three days later, Kurt returned to Powell to bring Jo and the new baby home. A blizzard had blown snow across the plains the day before his trip, piling up deep drifts along fences and the side of their house. The white sheets that Linda hung to dry on the outdoor clothesline before the storm were frozen solid.

Inside, her mother was greeted with a sink full of dirty dishes. She clutched the sleeping baby swaddled in a soft blue receiver blanket. Her eyes were moist, her face pale and contorted with worry lines.

Linda suddenly realized her mother didn't know about the frozen pipes. No running water since yesterday. She stepped close to Jo. "The water pipes are frozen, Mom."

"I can tell, honey. I'm sure they'll thaw soon."

"That's right," Kurt added. "A Chinook wind is supposed to come through in a day or two. That should warm things up and bring us back to normal."

Her mother retreated with the baby to the bedroom, searching for a clean diaper and an extra baby blanket. Linda and Jean trailed her, hoping for another glimpse of their baby brother.

～

That spring, before school let out, her parents talked about their need to get work outside of the valley. Her father had kept his job as a ranch hand for the Frakers through the winter, but he kept saying Mr. Fraker couldn't pay him enough to support their family. Her mother had mentioned how she might get a secretarial job in Powell or Cody so she could come home each night.

At supper one Sunday evening, Kurt finally spilled the beans about their new jobs. "You kids know your mother and I have been looking for work in this valley."

Christopher's cries interrupted him. The baby gasped for air between sucks and cried even louder. Jo cradled him in her arms and tried to calm him by poking the bottle into his mouth, but he had a stuffy nose from a bad cold.

Kurt glanced at Jo. "Maybe we'd better try this later."

Jo clutched the bottle in one hand, and leaned forward to stand up. "No. The kids are eager to hear from you. I'll rock the baby in the living room." As she left the room, the baby's raspy breathing and choked cries began to subside.

"Thanks, honey," Kurt sputtered. "Alright, kids. Let's try again. Your mother and I are starting new jobs soon. I've been hired to do road construction work in the Big Horns for the Anaconda Mine. I'll make good pay and that's hard to come by in this country."

Jean leaped up. "That's a long way from here, Daddy!"

"Yep, but I'll be coming home every night. Probably won't make supper with you kids though."

Linda sat quietly beside David, astonished by the news. She wondered what was coming next.

"Your mother has taken a secretarial job in Billings. As soon as we find her a small apartment, she can start work there. She'll have to leave here on Monday morning and come back home on Friday night. Now, we know that's going to be hard on everyone, especially your mother. After school lets out, David, you can work for the Frakers again this summer."

David shook his head left and right. "Come on, Dad. I want to make more than twenty-five cents an hour picking rocks off fields. That's all he's gonna pay me! I can get a mowing job like I did with you on the ranch and make more money."

"Those may be hard to get this year. Anyway, no one has leased our ranch yet, so they aren't looking for hired men."

David frowned. He had to figure out a different plan. "Look, Dad. I know how to drive a tractor with a baler. Mr. Fraker is just nervous because I don't have my driver's license yet. But I'm almost fourteen, and I've driven a tractor without a license before."

"You've got a point. I'll ask Harry about this next time I see him."

Linda hadn't said a word. She eyed her father as if to say, "What about me?" Finally, he turned to her.

"Linda. You'll be in charge of the house when your mother starts work. You know how to care for the baby, and you're a wonderful big sister. We'll need you to take care of them during the day until I get home at night."

"But, Dad. School won't let out for two more weeks."

"I know. Margie Weber says she'll watch you kids until then."

"That's good." She kept thinking about Christopher, although he was almost three months old now. Would she be able to take care of him on her own, without her mother around? She didn't have long to worry about that.

"Girls, better get the clothes off the line. It's almost dark."

The two sisters trudged outside together with the clothes basket, leaning forward to protect themselves against the biting wind.

13

THE PAINT JOB

Linda squeezed her mother hard around her waist, not wanting to let go. She got a whiff of her mother's skin, still damp from her morning shower. The fragrance of violets from the talcum powder dusted on her mother's shoulders and neck comforted her.

More than her mother's sweet smell caught her attention. Jo's reddish-blonde hair was pulled into a twist, held in place by several large bobby pins. Her freshly ironed, white cotton shirt was stiff from starch, and her new navy broadcloth skirt had box pleats instead of her usual gathered waist.

Linda was careful not to muss her up. She released her grip so Jean could say goodbye, too, suddenly shivering from the bite in the outside air.

She was finally ready for her mother's departure to Billings, eighty miles away. All weekend, her mother had been preparing her, showing her little things she needed to know to take care of the baby during the week—where she kept extra formula and how to sterilize the bottles if she ran out. She already knew how to do most everything, but her mother kept pointing things out, just in case.

"You can always run to Margie's house to get help."

Linda nodded. She could see the big cottonwood tree in the Weber's front yard. Margie Weber was their closest neighbor.

"And Christopher. If he gets sick . . ." Her voice trailed off.

"Don't worry, Mom, I'll take good care of him."

"I know you will, honey." She rubbed Linda's shoulder and drifted away.

"Jean and I are going to have a big surprise for you when you come home Friday night."

"Hmm. How about a hint?"

"No, Mom. You'll have to wait."

She sighed. Her slender figure trembled in the cold air.

Jean tugged on her mother's skirt, oblivious to the conversation. "I'll miss you, Mommy!"

Jo didn't seem to hear Jean. She shoved her arms into her tweed coat, pulling one side over the other to shut out the morning chill. At last, her eyes found the girls.

"You take good care of your baby brother and yourselves, too," she said absently. Her eyes darted away as she rummaged her purse for her car keys.

～

When her mother started the engine and pulled away, Linda was relieved that she hadn't choked up. After all, her mother had taken the job to help the family get on its feet again. She wiped her sleeve across her cheek to clear some tears and grabbed Jean's hand. As they trudged into the house, she started thinking how long it would be until Friday night.

As she pulled out a plastic bag full of corn flakes from the bottom kitchen cupboard and poured some into the bowls for her and Jean, she listened for Christopher's cries of hunger. Her mother had filled eight bottles of formula for him and put them into the fridge. All she had to do was put a bottle into a pan of hot water for five minutes and squirt a few drops of milk on her wrist to test the temperature.

By mid-morning, she started thinking about the surprise she

had promised her mother.

"Look at that, Jean." She pointed to the wall above the sofa in the living room.

"What's the matter?"

"It looks bad. Hasn't been painted in years. You can tell that."

Years of sun streaming through the living room window had bleached out the center part of the wall behind the couch. The rest was a slightly darker hue, like the cream that Mom used to skim off the fresh milk in the metal bucket each morning on the ranch.

Jean was unfazed. "It looks fine to me."

"Come on! Can't you tell that wall is faded and dirty? We could surprise Mommy by painting it before she comes home on Friday. David told me we have some yellow paint. We might have enough for the living room."

They found three gallons of paint in the cellar. Two had never been opened. It was white paint, not yellow, but they decided it would work anyhow. She and Jean could start painting after her father and David left for work on Tuesday.

She told her father about the painting project when he got home that night. He grinned. "Good idea, honey. Your mother will be tickled." He ordered David to bring the paint cans and brushes from the cellar for his sisters. After making a couple of runs, David staged everything on a big canvas tarp in the middle of the living room.

The next morning, after David left for the Fraker ranch and her father took off for his road job in the Big Horns, she called to Jean. "We've got to move this furniture out of here, Sissy."

Jean groaned. "All of it?"

"No, just the couch, chair and coffee table. We need to shove them against the wall so we can paint that one." She pointed to the front wall of the living room. It was the most complicated be-cause of two windows and the front door.

As they shoved one end of the couch across the linoleum floor, they heard the baby rustling in the crib. Linda peeked into her parents' bedroom. Sure enough. He was whimpering. He must be hungry again.

She handed Jean some butcher paper. "We can finish this af-ter I feed Christopher. Why don't you put some of this next to the wall to catch the paint drips?"

~

Linda hadn't expected Christopher's feeding to take so long. He was still wide-awake past his naptime. It was almost noon before he fell asleep in his crib and they could move the furniture again. They finished moving everything against the wall of their parents' bedroom so they could start painting.

Linda let Jean paint the bottom half of the wall while she stood on the yellow vinyl seat of a chrome kitchen chair to paint the top half. Jean used a three-inch brush, and Linda used the big paint roller. They were awkward at first. Some big globs of paint fell to the baseboard and the floor, but they were getting better at it. They made good progress until the baby woke up from his nap.

At first, they ignored his whimpers.

"Let's get this part done," Linda said. They had only a few more strokes to finish the wall next to the front door. As the baby's cries got louder and more insistent, the girls painted faster, trying to ignore him. Linda tried to calm him as she used up the fresh paint on her roller.

"I'm coming, sweet baby. We're almost done out here," she hollered. But the baby's cries didn't stop.

"Okay, he's not going to stop. I've got to give him a bottle now," she said. As she jumped off the chair, she remembered the bedroom door was blocked.

"Oh, my gosh!" She looked at Jean. "I can't get to Christopher. Help me shove this sofa back so I can get through the door."

The baby wailed until the doorway was clear and Linda scooped him up from the crib.

～

It was a long week. One day, while balancing on the chair and trying to dip the roller into the pan, Linda accidentally dumped paint on Jean's hair. Jean was furious.

"What do you think you're doing? How am I going to get this paint out of my hair?"

"We'll get it out later. We can't do it now because it'll take too long to rinse it out, and we need to finish this pan of paint."

"That's stupid! You better get this out of my hair now, before it gets hard," Jean yelled at her.

It took ten minutes of rinsing to get the paint out. "You're drowning me, Linda," Jean screamed. "That's enough!" She spit out the murky water and ran out of the room, her hair dripping wet.

By Friday, the girls had painted all the walls in the living room and their parents' bedroom. They tossed the old newspaper into the garbage can, bunched up the paint rags, and moved furniture back into place.

"Help me take these paint cans to the basement," Linda said, stopping Jean from drifting away from the job.

"Only if you promise you won't make me do one more chore before Mommy gets home."

"Alright. Stop complaining. I promise," Linda replied.

～

The afternoon stretched out forever. They made a big batch of oatmeal cookies but ended up eating most of the dough before baking some in the oven.

"I feel sick," Jean groaned.

"Me, too. That dough sure was good, though."

Hours before their mother arrived home, they had made their bed, picked up the house, and washed the dirty dishes from the cookie making. They put Christopher in his crib so Linda could braid Jean's hair special for the occasion.

It was dusk when they caught sight of the car lights beaming into the front room. The girls sprang for the door.

"Welcome home, Mommy!" they hollered outside.

Their mother clutched them to her chest. Linda felt like she couldn't breathe as Jean's warm body was squeezed in between. She held still until she felt her mother's gentle release.

The girls jostled one another for position, waiting for Jo's reaction to their paint job. But distracted by gurgling sounds coming from the bedroom, Jo dropped her purse and coat, and ran to get the baby.

"Mommy, wait! Don't you notice something's different?" Linda said. Her voice quivered with excitement as Jean proudly pointed to the living room wall.

Jo paused. Her eyes moved up and down the newly painted wall. She looked at the uneven rows of new paint, some barely covering the old paint, others opaque from three or four coats. The baseboard had blotches of paint here and there. Linda squirmed, wishing she could end the inspection.

"You girls painted these two rooms, didn't you? Is that your surprise, Linda?"

"Yep, it is. What do you think?" she asked breathlessly.

"It's very nice. Nice job, girls." She heaved a deep sigh. Her eyes welled with tears.

Jean shrugged her shoulders in bewilderment. "What's the

matter, Mommy?"

Linda pulled her arm and whispered, "I think Mommy's tired."

The girls trailed behind their mother as she edged her way again to the baby's crib. Their eyes fixed on Jo's back as she picked up the baby and smothered him with kisses.

Linda waved Jean away. "It's okay, Sissy. Mommy's had a hard week." But she knew it was about their paint job. Maybe they could do better next time.

14

SUMMER FRAGMENTS

A two-toned green '53 Chevy skidded to a stop at their front door. Linda rushed to the window and shoved back the dirty-white muslin drapes. Her stomach still churned like sour milk when strange cars drove up. As two nuns in long black robes swished their way to the doorstep, she released a big sigh of relief. It wasn't the bad man. She could open the door.

In keeping with tradition, each summer Sisters Mary Josephina and Mary Claire came from the convent in Powell to teach two weeks of vacation school at Our Lady of the Valley Catholic Church. The Sisters had promised Kurt and Jo they would pick up the girls each morning on their way to the church. The Glover's house was only a quarter mile off the main gravel road, on the final stretch of the twenty-five mile drive to the Clarks Fork Valley.

It had been six weeks since her mother had started work for the insurance company in Billings. Although the girls' paint job wasn't a big success, most everything else was fine. Kurt said she and Jean could go to the summer Catechism classes at the church so long as their chores were done each day. Mrs. Weber said she'd take care of the baby while the girls were gone.

Too bad David couldn't go with them this year. He was already working for Mickey Fraker, picking rocks off a field for twenty-five cents an hour. Although he had balked at the low pay, it was his first regular summer wage off the ranch, and it was a short drive from their new place in Badger.

"The Sisters are here," she shouted to Jean, letting the drape fall back. "Grab some diapers from the pile of clean clothes on Mom's bed and put them in the duffel bag."

Jean crammed cloth diapers along with bottles and extra baby clothes into the bag while Linda greeted the sisters.

"Good morning, Sister!" Linda said. "Come in."

"Thank you, dear," Sister Josephina said. She hiked up her black, floor-length garb to avoid tripping over it as she stepped inside. Her deep, hearty laugh made Linda forget about the starched white habit around her face. The habit reminded Linda of her father's beloved younger sister, Anna, a Holy Names nun. Sister Josephina was a head shorter and a lot chubbier than Sister Claire who towered behind her like a utility pole with long wiry arms.

"Jean's ready to go, but I have to take the baby around back to Mrs. Weber's," Linda said. She pulled Christopher from his crib and pressed him close to her chest, grabbed the duffel bag with her other hand, and set off for their neighbor's gray clapboard house.

~

The girls chatted non-stop with the sisters during the short drive to the church. They were too preoccupied to notice the rabbitbrush with their tiny yellow flowers sharing the wind-blown landscape with scattered clumps of thistles and sagebrush.

"Did you bring special treats for us this year?" Jean asked Sister Josephina.

"Sure enough. Plenty of Hershey's bars for everybody."

Jean bounced happily in the back seat, and Linda broke into a smile that showed the gap between her two front teeth, momentarily forgetting the flaw that made her self-conscious.

Jean poked her finger toward Linda's mouth, "I can see your gap!"

"Stop it, Jean," she exclaimed, covering her mouth with her hand.

Sister Josephina turned around to check on them. "Is something the matter?"

Linda dropped her hands and forced a smile. "Nothing, Sister. Jean was teasing me."

"Surely not about your lovely smile?"

Linda beamed and Jean stared out the window, ignoring the exchange altogether.

As they drove up the poplar-lined lane past the Baduras, the Catholic Church appeared on the barren hillside above the ranch compound, its white steeple reflecting the brilliant morning sun.

Plainer than her grandmother's church in eastern Oregon, this church didn't have the beautiful stained glass windows with the names of the Glover and Cleary families painted in several of them. And it didn't have the altar with big statues of Mary and Joseph on either side. But she liked the altar as it was, with a podium made out of light oak and with a simple hand-carved wooden cross in the middle.

In the basement hall, Linda joined a circle of girls she knew from the valley.

"What have you been doing this summer?" one of the girls asked. Regina, Buck Walter's daughter, spoke up. "I broke my first horse."

The girls' admiring glances encouraged her to continue.

"It wasn't so hard. The worst part was the first day, when I chased him around the corral a hundred times before I could get the rope around his neck!"

"You must've eaten some dust," Linda laughed.

"Yep. Right through my kerchief. What about you, Linda? Did you take Chestnut to Badger Basin with you?"

Linda's throat tightened. "Naw." Why'd Regina have to ask that? She felt heartbroken all over again. She seldom rode him, but the horse was like a member of the family. He had come all the way from Oregon with them in '54. But her dad had given him to a rancher near Belfry before they moved to Badger. Even though Chestnut was getting too old to ride the range, he was a gentle horse, especially tolerant of rambunctious kids. His new owner said Chestnut would be perfect for his family.

Linda's eyes darted to Edna, in hopes her best friend would take over, but she didn't say a word. "He couldn't come with us. There's no place for a horse in Badger, so my dad gave him away."

The girls gasped.

"That's too bad," Gretchen said at last. "You must miss him."

"Yeah. But I'm too busy taking care of my baby brother and my sister for my mom. She got a new job in Billings."

A hush took over the room. The girls' steely eyes bored into her for a longer explanation. Linda pressed back tears and walked away, praying to the nearby statue of the Virgin Mary that they would resume their horse-riding stories without her.

～

On Saturday nights, neighbors brought the whole family when they came for a visit. The Kowalski kids were the wildest. Marvin jumped onto the sofa cushions and over the back of the couch when they played hide-and-seek. This usually got all the kids sent outdoors, but nobody minded because they could chase each other around a circular path at the edge of the light cast by the gas flare.

Linda drew a line in the dirt path to mark the start line. "Okay. Get ready to race. I'll time you." She shouted the time from her father's stopwatch as each runner came across the finish line. Usually David or Marvin won, finishing the circle a few seconds ahead of the rest.

"I'm going to beat you next time," Jean insisted.

"No, you aren't," David said.

Jean poked a stick into the dirt. "You'll see. I'm going to beat you by the end of summer!"

Linda liked it when Jean stood up for herself. Being the youngest didn't bother her. She was determined, and she was fast. Still, Linda knew it would take Jean more than two months to beat David in a foot race.

~

Bob Marney picked up Kurt at five o'clock every morning for the two-hour drive to the Big Horns. It was usually dark when Kurt got home fourteen hours later—his face gritty with dirt and specks of ground rock from grading roads all day for the uranium mines.

He sat alone at the kitchen table and picked at the meatloaf and mashed potatoes that Linda had put aside for him. His slender figure leaned over the yellow ChromCraft table. The dull browns of his work clothes were a misfit with the bright yellow surface and wide silver band of the table.

"This sure is good, but I'm not very hungry tonight," he said, pushing his plate aside.

"But, Dad. I know meatloaf is your favorite."

She hated to give in. His cotton shirt looked a size too big for his chest, and his Levis hung from his hips instead of his waist.

David waited for Kurt to finish supper before he asked him about the grader. Earlier that winter, they had driven to Bozeman, Montana to buy a used road grader for his father's new job. "How's it working out, Dad?"

"Fine, Son. No breakdowns so far. Thank God for that. It's

mighty cold up there in the mountains."

"Is the noise and dust getting to you?"

His father looked far away, as if searching for an answer. "Sometimes it's bad. I have a hard time breathing those damned dust clouds from the mining operations nearby."

"Sounds real nasty." David shook his head sympathetically.

They fixed on each other while Linda cleared her father's plate from the table.

15

DECISION TIME

Linda stalled at the kitchen door, debating whether to interrupt her parents. They were locked in conversation. She felt the piercing strain in her mother's voice.

"We can't keep going like this. Look at you. You're wasting away."

"Long days. Not so much about the food I eat. I stuff a sandwich in my bag every morning, and Linda fixes me a good meal every night. 'Course, I don't always eat it."

He took a sip of coffee and set the mug back on the kitchen table.

"It's not worth your seventy dollars a week in road construction at the mine. And my weekly paycheck barely covers the apartment rent in Billings."

Linda's elbow hit the doorframe. She let out a muted squeal.

Jo twisted around. Her eyes flashed when she caught sight of Linda. "What are you doing up so early? It's only six thirty."

"I heard you talking."

"This is between your Dad and me."

Linda rubbed her sore elbow. Her mother finally noticed. "Did you hurt yourself?"

"Naw. It's starting to feel better."

Jo frowned at her. "Good. Now, I think you'd better go climb back into bed. I'll be here all weekend."

"Do you suppose we can go into town to shop today?" she

asked even though she knew better.

"No plans for that today. I brought some groceries home so we wouldn't have to drive to Powell this weekend."

"But, Mom. I need some new school clothes. School starts in a few weeks."

Her mother's face grew dark. "You have plenty of clothes to start school with."

Kurt threw his arms into the air. "There's no need for you to bother your mother about that."

She slipped away as quickly as she could, not wanting to add to their worries. New clothes could wait, but she knew another coat of shoe polish wasn't going to cover the cracks in the tops of her saddle shoes. Still, she dreaded having to wear the same pair of blue jeans that she wore all last school year. At least Jean had clothes that fit because they were hand-me-downs from her big sister.

~

Jo thumbed through the big stack of mail on the kitchen counter. She stopped when she came to an envelope postmarked from California.

"It's from Ava."

"Again?"

"She's having a hard time getting over Francy's death."

Linda shrugged her shoulders. "It makes me sad to think about her, too. But they still have Sarah, don't they?" She remembered Francy talking about her older sister when they visited the ranch.

"Yes, but Sarah's married now. She hasn't lived with Ava and Charlie since high school. She hopes you can come visit her sometime this year," Jo said.

"She does?" Linda fumbled for reasons why they would want

her to visit when Francy wasn't there anymore.

"It might make sense, if your dad and I decide to move to California this fall."

Linda jerked around, startled by her mother's disclosure, but Jo kept her eyes fixed on opening another envelope. "We haven't made up our minds yet. I don't want to keep driving to Billings every Monday and leaving you kids. It's too hard on all of us."

"I know, Mom."

"We can't stay in Badger Basin through another winter. Your dad needs a better job too, closer to home."

"Where would we go?"

"Maybe Modesto. Live with your aunt Kathy and uncle John. They said we could stay with them for a while until your dad and I find jobs. We promised to let them know."

"Oh." Her mind swirled with confusing thoughts.

"Do you remember when they visited us on your grandparents' ranch in Oregon? You were just a little girl then."

"I think so." She tried hard to remember their faces. "Don't they have three or four kids? Won't it be too crowded?"

"I suppose. But we wouldn't stay there for long."

"Is that why you might send me to Ava's?"

"Well, it would be a help. And your aunt wants you to stay with her. She remembers how you and Francy took to each other during their visit. They have a big house. Plenty of room."

"Does David know?"

"Not yet. Your father and I have a lot to think about. No sense in getting you kids worked up over something that might not happen." She returned to opening envelopes and paying bills.

Later, Linda caught David in the bathroom washing his hands for supper. She told him as much as she could remember from the morning conversation. "It's top secret, David. Everything I just told you!" she hissed.

"Okay, okay. But what else did Mom say? How are we all

going to fit into their house?"

"She said it's going to be crowded. But she and Dad haven't decided yet. They'll let Uncle John and Auntie Kathy know soon."

"Too bad you didn't ask Mom more questions when you had the chance. The folks won't bring this up again. You know that."

"Yes, they will. I bet real soon." She knew he was right, but his smugness annoyed her. She dipped her hands under the faucet for a quick wash and flung the damp towel down as she rushed to catch up with him.

"So how're we going to move to California without any money?" David asked.

"How would I know? Come on, David. All I know is I might stay with Ava and Charlie for awhile."

"What?"

"Mom said Ava wants me to come visit them."

"Visit them? That's got to be crazy when they are still crying over Francy."

"I know it. But Ava's been writing Mom a lot lately. Mom even said they're thinking about adopting another child."

"Adopt *another child*? What do you mean?"

"Didn't you know? Francy and Sarah were both adopted." She suddenly felt superior to him. Finally, she knew something her older brother didn't know.

But David had a quick comeback. "Whoa! Maybe they'll adopt you, Sis."

"You wish! I'm going to ask them to take me to Hollywood. I want to meet a movie star like Jane Russell or Loretta Young." She gazed out the window.

"You're dreaming, Linda. You can't just go to Hollywood and run into a movie star. The closest you'll get to Loretta Young is the eight-by-ten glossy picture tacked on your bedroom wall."

He stomped the floor to reinforce his point and leaned toward her. "Listen, we need to know what's really going to happen if we move to California. We can't pick up and leave without a plan. Dad's gonna have to have a job. Mom, too."

~

Linda kept thinking about what David had said. Maybe her parents did have a plan. After all, they had moved to Wyoming all the way from Oregon three years before and they must have had a plan then. But this time felt different. Moving from their Quonset house in Badger Basin to California seemed like a big stretch of unknown.

Her father was so tired every day, and her mom was around only on the weekends. Maybe she would have to get Jean to help with the packing. How far was Ava and Charlie's place from Hollywood? Could her aunt and uncle take her to MGM so she could meet a real movie star? She ran out of the room to find Jean.

"Jean! Can you imagine going to Hollywood?"

Jean was wiping the kitchen floor to clean up the milk she had spilled.

"What are you talking about?"

Linda stopped. Jean didn't even know that they might move. "Oh, nothing. I was thinking about how neat it would be to meet some movie stars."

"You're dreaming, Linda!"

That's what David said, too. It was better than worrying about how they would make this move.

~

Three weeks later, her parents packed their belongings into the bed of the pickup that Kurt had outfitted with a steel rack and left for California. David got to ride shotgun with his dad in the truck. Jean and Linda rode alongside Jo in the car. Christopher was in the backseat surrounded by pillows and blankets and coats.

Their departure marked the family's three-year anniversary of their move to Wyoming.

III

MODESTO, CALIFORNIA 1957

16

JOURNEY TO CALIFORNIA

The road from Cody to West Yellowstone narrowed as it wound along the Shoshone River to the Buffalo Bill Dam. It snaked through narrow tunnels blasted by dynamite sticks jammed into the granite mountainside. Stacked waist-high along the roadside, massive boulders kept cars from plunging into the deep blue reservoir far below.

It was late afternoon when Kurt saw the sign for Old Faithful. Time to get off the road. He throttled down the yellow GMC truck and pulled into a campground along the Yellowstone River. Jo pulled up alongside in the Ford sedan.

"Looks good to me," she shouted to him.

The kids bolted from the vehicles and chased each other around the campground.

"Okay. That's enough," Kurt barked. "You woke the baby up, and you're causing a dust storm. Pull out the sleeping bags and tent from the back."

David started flinging sleeping bags to the ground. One bag struck Jean's stubby legs from behind, and she fell forward, sprawling in the dirt. "Sorry, Sissy," he said, but she spat dirt at him as he grabbed her hand.

Linda rushed at her brother. "Stop it, David. You're not the boss!"

But Kurt carried on. "Your mother and I will sleep on the ground over there." He pointed toward the area behind the fire pit. "You girls can sleep in the tent."

Jo brought Christopher over. He looked like a wriggling butterball perched on her right hip, his tiny feet barely extending beyond the legs of his overalls.

Jean poked her finger into his pudgy belly. "Oose goose." He squirmed and rewarded her with a giggle.

"Where's he going to sleep?" she asked her mother.

"In the back seat of the car. He'll be nice and toasty with all those pillows and blankets."

Jo set up the Coleman stove on one end of the picnic table and found a can opener for the chili beans and Vienna sausages. It was almost dark when she called them to the table.

~

Camping at Yellowstone was the highlight of their trip to eastern Oregon. The second day's drive was a long ten hours across Idaho, through the Craters of the Moon, to Boise. The last hundred-mile stretch took them through the Owyhee Mountains, over the Idaho state line into Oregon, and on to the family ranch.

Kurt honked as he pulled off Highway 95 into the gravel entry to the ranch. The wide lane extended past the side of the house to the corral, where the weathered barn stood at the back of the compound. A row of tall, craggy cottonwood trees lined the west side, shading the two-story house from the high desert sun.

The plain, white-painted house reminded him of their Wyoming ranch house, except for the familiar bumpy front lawn that was full of crabgrass and gopher holes. Mother had often bragged about how the house was built in the late 1800s with square nails.

Kurt's parents had lived in the house since their marriage in 1916 and all four of their children had been born there. His mother had lived alone on the ranch since his dad's death last winter, a month before Christopher was born.

As short and round as ever, his mother waved at them with her kitchen apron from the back porch. Her cropped, silver-gray hair was a mass of tiny curls, a sure sign that she had gotten a recent perm from Pauline, the town's only hairdresser. The kids rushed to greet their grandmother as Jo gathered Christopher, and Kurt grabbed a pile of clothes and shoes from the backseat.

~

At daybreak, Kurt went down to the kitchen to put the aluminum coffee pot on the cast iron stove. He stuck in a couple chunks of dry wood to rekindle the fire, all the while hearing his mother rustling around in her bedroom, on the other side of the short, narrow door to the kitchen. It always took her several minutes to tie all those corset strings, tightly cinching her waist in place. Gave him time to think more about Sam, whether he ought to touch bases with him before leaving town.

It hadn't been that long ago, in January, that they were together at his dad's funeral. They'd had a brief exchange, but Kurt hadn't mentioned how they'd moved off the Wyoming ranch to Badger Basin the fall prior. Still, seeing Sam again was the last thing he wanted to do. He didn't want to discuss his failure to make a go of the Wyoming ranch. It would only confirm Sam's view of him as inept, incapable of making good business decisions. The whole experience had burned him out. No use sharing that he had vowed never to do ranching again. He didn't have much time this trip anyway. He'd see Sam on a future visit. Give himself time to get settled in California.

~

The only phone in the house hung in the dining area outside the kitchen door. Toward noon, Kurt and Jo squeezed together on the church pew that his mother had pilfered from St. Bernard's Catholic Church in exchange for her weekly laundry services for the local priest. Kurt dialed the number for Jo's sister and brother-in-law in Modesto, California.

"Hey, John. Kurt here." Kurt yelled into the phone. It was a party line shared by neighbor ranchers. "That you, Kathy? I've got Jo here beside me."

Before the call, Kurt ordered the kids outside, but Linda kept sketching on a piece of butcher paper that covered most of her grandmother's art table. Her father didn't seem to mind. And she wasn't bothered by the big picture of the bleeding heart of Jesus hanging over her head. She'd gotten used to the gory print. It was one of many religious pictures on the living room walls that seemed part of the furniture.

"No, John. Absolutely not! We know you have a crowded household. No point in our making it worse by bringing all our kids, too." Silence filled the room. Linda held her drawing pencil mid-air, waiting for her father to continue.

Kurt's voice got louder. "Look. David and Jean can stay with my folks here on the ranch for a few weeks until school starts. Ava and Charlie have invited Linda to stay with them in Beaumont. I'll take her down there after we get to Modesto. That'll mean the baby and us at your place."

Linda felt like a rush of cold air had hit her. She bolted outside to find David, passing Jean as she shot through the wood-framed screen door before it whapped shut behind her. She spotted David balancing with one leg on the rope swing knotted around a giant branch of the cottonwood tree in the backyard.

"What's the matter?" he asked. They huddled together on the back porch, perched side by side on the cement pad that their Grandpa had poured before the family moved to Wyoming. Their names, along with the other grandchildren's, were etched in the concrete.

"Do you think you'll get to Modesto by the time school starts?" she asked.

"I don't know. Dad hasn't said anything to me. But I guess they have a plan, after all." He grabbed a broken tree branch and poked it into a crack in the cement.

"What do you mean?"

"They've got a plan for sending you to southern California with Mom's aunt and uncle, don't they?"

"Yeah."

"And a plan for me and Jean to stay here with Grandma?"

She nodded.

"The weird thing is you barely know those people, Sissy. Being relatives doesn't make them family."

"I guess so. But they must be rich. Mom said Gorgeous George stays there sometimes, too. People come there to see him and his purple turkeys."

"Purple turkeys? You're making up stories!"

"That's what Mom told me."

He shoved the stick further into the cracked cement, breaking it in half. "No matter. Bet he's not going to pay any attention to you."

"You're just being mean!"

"He doesn't know you from Adam."

"So what? I bet you Ava and Charlie will take me to Hollywood."

He smirked at her. She kicked the broken sticks off the cement slab onto the lawn and sprinted for the back door.

~

Her parents had made up their minds. The more she thought about what she'd told David, the more sure she became that Ava and Charlie would take her to Hollywood. She would ask Charlie to take her picture with a star—proof to show her brother and sister when she saw them again. Gorgeous George must know some movie stars, or maybe some TV stars. Either way, she'd be home in a few weeks; her photos would amaze David and Jean.

She danced a jig right there in the tiny hallway outside the bathroom. Everything would turn out okay.

~

At supper that night, the family sat down at the extended oak table that Grandma has accepted from a boarder years ago as payment for his lengthy stay in an upstairs bedroom. With a final flourish of activity by Jo and Grandma, bowls filled to the top with fried chicken and mashed potatoes, along with a huge rhu- barb pie, were delivered from the kitchen. The kids sat against the wall on the church pew.

Grandma stood at the head of the table and called for the family to say Grace. Her commanding voice rang out in the room, "*Bless us O Lord, and these thy gifts, which we are about to receive, from thy bounty, through Christ, our Lord. Amen.*" It was a familiar re- frain to the returning family members.

After supper, the adults settled into conversation. When Grandma revealed she was negotiating with the BLM to renew grazing rights for the cattle, she grabbed Kurt's attention. It sig- naled she was taking charge of the ranch after Grandpa's death. But Linda wondered if her parents were ever going to bring up the subject that was on her and David's minds. Finally. Her father started from scratch, as if she hadn't heard his booming phone voice earlier.

"Your mother and I talked with your uncle John and aunt Kathy today. They said it's fine for us to stay at their house. But there's not enough room for all of us. David, you and Jean are going to stay here for a few weeks until school starts in the fall."

Linda leaned across the table toward her father. She knew what was coming.

"After we get to Modesto, I'll drive you to southern California where Ava and Charlie live. Ava told your Mom they would love to have you."

Jo nervously swept her wavy hair away from her face. "Yes. Ava said you could sleep in Francy's room, Linda."

Linda shuddered. The idea of sleeping in Francy's bed gave her the creeps, but she couldn't say that to her mother. She pictured Francy waving goodbye from the backseat of the Oldsmobile the day they left the Wyoming ranch. Her parents waved through the front windows until their car disappeared over the hill. On that bright summer morning, Ava and Charlie could never have imagined losing their saucy daughter only a year later.

~

The daylong ride from eastern Oregon across Nevada to California was hot and sweaty under the relentless desert sun. Kurt drove alone in the pickup, while Linda sat next to her mother on the cloth seat of the '54 Ford, holding Christopher in her lap.

Close to midnight, when they turned onto Glendale Avenue in Modesto, Linda shook her tingly legs awake. As her mother wrapped the baby in a blanket, Kurt parked the truck along the curb across the street.

Light filtered through the open front door, illuminating the late night visitors for Kathy and John. Linda stood in the shadow sizing up her aunt and uncle while the adults exchanged a flurry of hugs and backslaps. John was shorter than Kurt, but equally skinny, and he had the same upright military pilot stance. She remembered that both of them had flown planes for the Army in the Pacific in World War II. Unlike Jo, Kathy had dark brown hair, but she shared her sister's slender shape and soft brown eyes.

Kathy finally noticed Linda, glancing at her pre-teen frame. "You've grown several inches since we last saw you!" It had been more than three years since their families were together at her grandparents' ranch in eastern Oregon. She patted her niece on the shoulder. "Here. Let me show you where you'll sleep tonight. You must be tired."

Kathy had made up the sofa bed in the living room, complete with a square couch pillow covered with a fresh pillowcase. Linda tucked her tennis shoes under the bed and pulled back the cover, but when John walked by to show her parents the house, she trailed them down the hall.

"We've cleared a shelf for your things," John said, as he held open the bathroom door. Heaped in the corner of the bathroom were damp towels, and kids' dirty clothes were scattered on the floor. Linda knew her mother would never let a bathroom be this messy.

"Where are Anthony and Benny sleeping?" Kurt said. He glimpsed across the hall at the boys' school pictures posted above their beds. Filled with Tinker Toys and play balls, a square wooden box sat in the corner of the room.

"In our room."

"We don't want to put you out, John," Jo said.

"Not at all," he insisted. "Not at all."

～

After John left for work the next day, Kurt grasped the horizontal bars on the back metal rack above the truck bed, lifted it overhead, and leaned it against the pickup. He pulled down the tailgate, hopped onto the truck bed, and started tossing boxes, bags of clothing, and blankets to the gaggle of children below him eager to help out. They stacked the boxes at the back of the carport to leave space for the two cars.

Dust flew. The clamor drew neighbor kids, too, some on roller skates and bicycles. It felt like their move to Badger Basin, except there were lots of kids around, and David and Jean weren't there.

As soon as the last box was out of the truck, Linda ran to shore up clothes bags piled high alongside some boxes. A few neighborhood kids hung around, poking around the boxes.

"Get away from those boxes!" she bossed. She sounded like her dad. Maybe she was getting nervous about going to Ava and Charlie's.

~

Kurt and Linda left early Friday morning for southern California. Linda carried a half-full duffel bag and a small brown vanity case that Kathy had given her for the trip.

Her mother was the last of the family parade to say goodbye. "Have fun, honey. Say hello to Ava and Charlie for me."

"You'll let me know when you and Dad get a house?"

"Sure." She promised. "We'll let you know."

But Linda had an uneasy feeling about her mother's subdued response. "Can I give Christopher another hug goodbye?"

"Here you go." Her mother handed him over.

Linda held him tightly and nuzzled his neck. She smelled his sweetness, the taste of his skin. "Bye-bye, baby. Don't forget your big sister." She blinked back tears as she passed him back to her mother.

They were finally on their way. Her father said it would take six hours to reach the turkey ranch on the edge of the Palm Desert. Linda smiled up at him. This was her chance to have him all to herself, but he was already lost in thought. Before long, the drone of Highway 99 filled the small cab.

17

DREAMS OF HOLLYWOOD

Hot air from the superheated asphalt poured through the open windows of the pickup. Highway 99 through the Central Valley was a blur of golden fields for miles and miles. Only salvage yards, used car lots, and strip malls on the outskirts of towns interrupted the parched landscape. Linda squinted at the heaps of salvaged metal car parts as they passed a junkyard, and stared at big billboards advertising cigarettes and sleek new Chevrolets and Fords.

The billboards for Mammoth Orange and Giant Orange roadside stands featuring people sipping icy orange juice and eating big, juicy hamburgers connected with her growling stomach. Close to noon, she spotted a stand shaped like a giant orange.

"Can we stop now, Dad?" She shook him out of his road trance.

"Sure. It's getting too damned hot!"

They ate lunch at the lone picnic table shaded by the slanted corrugated metal roof rigged to provide shelter to the food stand. Her father devoured his burger and cold orange drink before pulling a cigarette from his pack of Pall Malls in his shirt pocket. As he smoked, the puffs blended with the shimmering heat waves surrounding them. She scarfed down the burger, certain that he'd want to go the minute he finished his smoke.

After the lunch stop, the four-hundred-mile trip felt longer with each mile. Her dad stopped only to fill up the gas tank and give her a potty break.

"We'll be there about dinner time. Your mother says Ava's a good cook. Bet she'll fix something you like."

"Like what?"

He didn't answer. Besides, the constant roar of passing trucks and semis made it hard to hear.

~

As the hours passed, she began to ask him questions.

"Mom said Uncle Charlie runs the ranch for Gorgeous George. Does George live there, too?"

"No, but Charlie says he visits from time to time. That's 'cause he's divorced. And he's probably gone a lot for his TV wrestling matches. But this place must give him a nice getaway."

Her parents had said George made a lot of money from the TV shows. They laughed about his bleached hair and gold-plated hairpins that he threw to the ladies from the ring.

"Does he really wear purple robes that have sequins on them?"

"Yep. He wears fancy robes into the ring. The crowd loves it when he struts in, especially the women. They scream and act silly. It's just a show, but it makes him a lot of money."

"Why don't you try that, Dad?"

He acted shocked by her question. "Hey! I'm a rancher, not a showman like George."

"I know. Anyway, I'd be so embarrassed if you did that." She paused. "But, Dad, how long am I going to stay there?"

"Where?" He seemed distracted.

"You know. At Ava's."

"Hard to say. A few weeks. Maybe until Christmas. Enough time for us to get jobs and find a house that's big enough."

She withered inside. First time she'd heard mention of Christmas. Was he losing confidence in getting a job?

"But, Daddy. That's a long time from now!"

He glanced down at her, considering his response.

"What the hell!" he yelled, and hit the brakes. An eighteen-wheeler had swerved into their lane. She slid across the bench seat and slammed against the door as Kurt's pickup screeched to a halt on the shoulder of the highway.

"You okay, honey?"

"Guess so." She wore a brave face, though her shoulder ached.

"Nothing broken?"

She raised her shoulder to test it out. "It aches a little bit. But I think it's okay. Guess that guy wasn't looking ahead?"

"Yeah. I bet he drifted asleep at the wheel. These long-haul guys are on the road day and night."

They watched the big rig roll forward again and slowly regain speed.

She was quiet after that. The silence gave her time to study him. She wanted to remember exactly what he looked like so she wouldn't get too lonely after he left her at the ranch. She'd inherited his gray-green eyes and high cheekbones; otherwise, David and Jean looked more like him—his olive complexion and thick curly black hair. He was tall and skinny and walked faster than anyone she knew. She had to run to keep up with him, whether walking across the fields on the ranch or crossing the street in California.

~

They pulled into Charlie and Ava's place in Beaumont at five o'clock. Kurt turned off the motor and honked the horn. The sun was still high in the sky, and the vinyl seat cover was so hot it stuck to her bare legs as she wiggled out.

Ava flung open the back screen door and ran to greet them, Charlie trailing behind. Her aunt was petite, even in stacked heels. She wore a sleeveless white blouse and black pedal pushers that showed off her slim figure. Her black hair had a swath of gray at the temple. It was shorter than when they had visited the Wyoming ranch two years ago. Slathered with bright red lipstick, her full lips contrasted with her pale white face. Thick globs of black mascara sat on her eyelashes.

"Linda, dear. We're so glad you're here," Ava said. She smooched Linda's left cheek and wrapped her arms around her. Linda squirmed as the red lipstick smeared across her face. She wished Ava wasn't quite so personal. After all, she barely knew her.

"Do you want to get your suitcase before we go inside?" Ava said.

"I guess so." For a moment, she had forgotten that she would stay there after her dad left the next morning.

"Need some help?" Charlie asked. He stood next to Kurt, matching him in height, but thicker at the waist. Carefully combed to one side, his thinning, light brown hair concealed a large forehead.

"Naw. I can get it," she said. She pulled her canvas duffle bag out of the dusty pickup bed. "Here it is." She lifted it high to show her aunt.

"Is that all your luggage, dear?" Ava said.

"Yes."

"Okay then. You can put it in Francy's bedroom. I've got it cleaned up for you."

From the carport, they stepped down to the gleaming white kitchen that featured cupboards with crystal knobs and pearly-white Formica counters. Two steps lower, in the living room, a sleek, curved sofa faced an outdoor patio filled with palm trees and leafy bushes.

It was the fanciest house Linda had ever seen. She tried hard not to stare at everything.

"I call it California ranch," Ava pointed out as they followed her down the long breezeway to the bedroom suites.

Linda peered through the large screens that framed the carpeted walkway on either side—the patio garden on her left, and the circular driveway, lined with palm trees, on her right.

As they entered the hallway with bedrooms at either end, Ava escorted Linda to her new bedroom, complete with her own bathroom. She swept back the floor-length drapes to show the manicured lawn outside her window, and opened the folding doors to the closet.

"I've pushed back Francy's clothes so you have room to hang yours."

Linda was shaken. Why were Francy's clothes still there after all this time?

Ava sensed her unease. "Her clothes may be too big for you, but you're welcome to wear them if they fit."

Linda winced. How would Francy feel about her cousin taking over her bedroom—the clothes, the shoes, the record player? The colorful bedspread, in red and white stripes, matched the drapes covering the picture window. The wall was full of Francy's school photos—an official school picture for each school year through the eighth grade. Covered with school memorabilia, her bulletin board included Girl Scout pins and a set of purple and gold cheerleader pompoms slung over the top corner.

"Thanks, Ava. Linda appreciates it," her father filled in for her.

Ava smiled at her. "Why don't you put the duffel bag on top of the bed for now? You can unpack after dinner."

Linda schlepped the bag onto the bedspread. "This is a real nice room, Auntie," she said at last.

"Glad you like it! Now I've got to get dinner started before your dad and Charlie complain about being starved."

～

At dinner, Linda listened to Ava and Charlie reminisce about their trip to Wyoming the summer of 1955. They mentioned Francy several times, as if she hadn't died in that terrible hiking accident last year. Kurt nodded from time to time as if he were listening to every word.

It was past nine o'clock when she pulled the first things out of her duffel bag. Almost everything she brought from Wyoming was there: a couple of dresses for church and school, her Levis, two T-shirts and a long-sleeve shirt, a heavy wool coat, and her saddle shoes for school.

She put her special folder of paper dolls on the tall walnut dresser and searched for a place on Francy's bulletin board to tack the glossy photos of movie stars taken from her bedroom wall in Wyoming. They reminded her of her hopes to visit Hollywood. She finally crawled under the covers and put her head on the down pillow. Jean will be amazed, she thought. She won't believe my new bedroom.

～

At breakfast, she slurped milk from a bowl of corn flakes while her dad drank his coffee.

"You're going to have fun here, Linda. Ava and Charlie will take good care of you."

"I'll miss you, Daddy!"

"Ditto, honey. I'll be back before you know it."

"I know," she said, forcing a smile.

"Ava says the school has over a hundred students. That's a

lot more than Clark had." He chuckled at the comparison. He kept reminding her that she would be in sixth grade—at the top of the heap. She'd turned eleven in April. That made her and David only a year apart because he wouldn't turn thirteen until October.

His departure came quicker than she thought. Kurt thanked Ava and Charlie for the last time and grabbed Linda's hand on his way to the pickup. He held her hand tight until he swung into the cab.

She kept waving goodbye until the pickup was a hazy dot on the horizon. "It's going to be a long trip," she said aloud. Her father wouldn't have to take a freeway exit until he reached the outskirts of Modesto in the Central Valley.

"Yes, it is," Ava said. "But your dad always enjoys a long drive."

A lump came into her throat as she walked back into the house with Ava and Charlie. She suddenly felt very alone.

18

KURT LOOKS FOR WORK

Quiet pervaded the house before the morning crush. Only the hum of the fridge broke the silence. Soon everyone would be fighting for the only bathroom. Kurt scooped coffee grounds from the bright red MJB can into the aluminum percolator. He shoved the top down, turned the electric burner on high, and waited for the coffee to start perking.

He wanted to catch John before he left for work to ask him about seasonal jobs in the Central Valley. John was a chemist at Gallo, the biggest winery in the Valley. He had started with the company after graduating with a degree in oenology from Oregon State in 1949.

"I like the security," John had said. "Growing family and all."

Back then, John and Kathy had only their first child. Now they had four, like him and Jo. But Kurt's life had taken a different turn. He had just a year and a half of college under his belt at Oregon State University when he was drafted into the Army in '42 at age 21. He knew that his experience flying lightweight, observation planes in the Army field artillery, and his work in the rock crushing business after he returned from the Philippines, wouldn't count for much now.

It would take him two to three years to finish a bachelor's degree in civil engineering, or to get certified to fly commercial airplanes. No question about it. He needed some cold, hard cash

now to get the family back together. He didn't like being depend-
ent on Jo's family. And he really missed the kids.

~

John finally popped into the kitchen, dressed for work in his dark
gray slacks and white short-sleeved dress shirt. A dark blue,
skinny tie draped over his right shoulder.

"Morning, Kurt. I smelled that coffee down the hall. You're
up early. Must be the rancher in you."

"'Been getting up early all my life. Here you go. Fresh brew."
He handed John a mug. "I thought I'd get a jump on the unemployment office downtown. Guess you know I haven't had any
luck with locating a farm in this Valley that could use my ranch
management know-how. Hard to believe that two weeks have
gone by already. Figured I better check out the help-wanted post-
ings for day laborers on the farms around here."

"That's a good place to start. August is peak harvest season
for the orchards—apricots, peaches, and plums. Not sure what
they pay, though."

John looked his brother-in-law up and down. "You've got
quite a load on your shoulders, with your kids scattered and all."

Kurt nodded. "Yep. With a little luck, I expect we can get our
own place before Christmas."

"Luck, and a little of your Glover charm will get you there."

Kurt felt his shoulders tense up. "So you think I'm not trying
hard enough?" His steely, gray eyes fixed on John. After all, John
didn't know what it was like to lose a ranch. He had the good
fortune to have graduated from college and brought home a
monthly paycheck ever since.

John shrank back, abashed by Kurt's outburst. "Come on
now, buddy. I have faith in you. Can't forget what you did in
flying those grasshoppers in the Pacific, for one. Took guts."

Kurt gazed at the trellis laden with clusters of vine-ripened grapes outside the kitchen window. "Do you suppose Gallo might have any seasonal work for a guy like me?" It felt good to change the subject.

"It's a little early for the harvest work at wineries around here. The grapes will be ready in another five to six weeks if the hot weather holds. Then there'll be plenty of work to do through the fall."

Kurt patted John on the shoulder. "Good to know. Maybe by then I won't need it. I found the unemployment office in the Yellow Pages. Can you give me directions downtown?"

John pulled a city map from the drawer, smoothed it flat on the kitchen counter, and pointed to the box-like grid of city streets. Kurt grunted his thanks and shifted gears again. "Are there orchards east of here that might be hiring?"

"Don't know. Your best bet is to take Yosemite Road east toward Sonora Pass. Plenty of small farms and orchards in that area." He folded the map again and handed it to Kurt. "Good luck today," he said, placing his empty mug back on the counter.

They walked out the front door together. Kurt took off in his GMC pickup, still coated with dust from their long trip west, and John left in his green Studebaker. Kurt glanced back at John's car. It reminded him of something. Yes, the guy who had tried to hurt the girls in Wyoming. Kurt never found out if he drove a Studebaker, but the sight of that car made him shudder all over again.

~

Kurt strode into the unemployment office when they opened the doors at eight thirty. Men hungry for work pressed forward to take a number and check out the bulletin boards. He scanned the crowd. Mostly Mexican Braceros, laborers with Green Cards, who seemed familiar with the daily routine. Plenty of nervous faces fervently searching for a friendly employment officer.

He studied the bulletin board, jotting down names and addresses of orchards that needed day laborers to pick the ripe fruit. Peak season. The Tillie Lewis Cannery on 9th Street also advertised for help on the food processing lines. Paid a dollar seventy-five an hour. Better than nothing. He decided to check it out. It was only a few miles east.

Kurt came away from the plant discouraged. It was cavernous. Full of workers on long canning lines. He couldn't see himself confined indoors to a food processing line all day. Fresh air felt damned good, summer and winter. Even in the winter blizzards that slammed their ranch, he would venture outside long enough to check on the livestock every day.

He hadn't picked fruit for a living before, but he liked that it was outdoor work. He remembered their apple orchard a quarter mile from the ranch house. Lots of old crab apple trees. Every September, he and Jo would spend the better part of a morning shaking those trees. The kids would scamper around to scoop up the booty, filling buckets for the return home.

Kurt walked toward the tall, spindly man whose oversized T-shirt was shoved inside dirty painter's overalls stained with peach juice. Sweat dripped from the man's forehead onto his beaky nose. He pulled his wrinkled, white handkerchief from his pants pocket to catch the drops, swiping his forehead.

"How much do you pay for pickin'?" Kurt asked.

"A dollar fifty an hour or by the piece. Ten flats of peaches, quality pick, brings you five dollars. Fifty cents a flat. Depends on how fast you are at picking and packing without bruising the merchandise. And how much you want to make."

While Kurt studied the situation, Mexican laborers walked around him with their empty buckets, heading for their designated rows to begin the picking. Ladders had been placed on most rows to reach fruit near the treetops. Kurt mumbled to himself.

"Got a question?" the man asked.

"No, sir. This is the first place I've stopped. Not sure if this work suits me."

He walked back to his pickup out front. Goddamned fleecing operation. No better than a job some Mexican could get fresh across the border. He didn't mind hard work. But it irritated him to think some guy running an apple orchard would offer him less than he made as a hired hand to Mickey Fraker last summer after leaving the ranch—a ranch he'd managed on his own until things fell apart. A ranch twenty times this size with livestock and an apple orchard on the side.

He spent the day driving to other orchards he'd written down on the note card. Same story each place: pay by the piece or by the hour. Late afternoon, he pulled into the front yard of a farm on Leek Road, a half mile south of Yosemite Boulevard. He hailed the first man who looked like he might manage the place.

Kurt introduced himself. "I just moved my family here from Wyoming. I need a job. I can do anything you might need done around here."

The man shook Kurt's hand. "Hank Staples. Sounds like you've got a story there."

"Yep. I ran a twelve hundred acre cattle ranch in Wyoming. Turned upside down when livestock prices took a dive. But there's no time to dwell on losses when you have a family to feed."

Hank shrugged his shoulders. "Appreciate your predicament. Sorry to say we got nothing suitable right now. My brother moved here not long ago from Nebraska. He had a farm there that failed. Sounds similar to what you've gone through. He's helping me out till he gets his feet on the ground."

Kurt reached for words. "Got a piece of scrap paper? I'll give you my number in case you need more help."

Staples tore a piece from his scruffy notebook and handed him a pencil. Kurt scribbled a note and pressed it into the man's palm. His long legs felt like lead weights as he plodded back to his truck.

"Hey, good luck," the man shouted from behind.

"Thanks," Kurt said, not looking back.

It wasn't like him to walk this slowly. He could cross the back forty acres on the ranch in a few minutes when he needed to fix an irrigation ditch before a summer downburst, or get to the ranch house for lunch.

When he shut the door to his pickup, the whole cab seemed to quiver. It was his last stop for the day. He had to figure out what he would tell the two families waiting for him at John and Kathy's house.

~

He slipped quietly into the noisy household. In the kitchen, Jo helped Kathy get dinner. She looked up from peeling carrots and flashed him a hopeful smile.

"How'd it go, honey?" She dropped the paring knife on the countertop and crossed the center aisle to peck his cheek. He squeezed her tight. He wished he had some good news for her.

"I ended up talking to three orchard managers and a farmer who has a big spread down the road, off Yosemite past Empire. You know, the little town just past the railroad crossing?"

She nodded. "Did you get a bite on a job?"

Kurt's smile concealed his shame. He couldn't bear her hopeful look. Drove him crazy not to have something positive to report. Any job would be better than having to tell her he came up empty-handed. "The farmer was real friendly. Told me he'd take me on, except he has hired his brother who lost his farm in Nebraska this past year."

But she saw through his smile. "There's gotta be another farmer in the vicinity who needs a man with your experience," she said, her voice gritty with determination.

He patted her shoulder but she pulled away.

"We've got to figure something out," she said. "It's rough being here all day in such tight quarters, though Kathy tries her best to be sweet to us."

Christopher crawling through the kitchen door distracted them. Kurt couldn't resist the little guy. He swept him into his arms and tickled his round belly.

"Don't worry, honey," he said. But his words echoed through the room. Jo wasn't in listening range.

~

John grilled him again later that evening. He kept asking why Kurt hadn't taken the job at the cannery. "Hey, it's not so bad. Kathy worked there last summer. She earned enough to afford the down payment for this house."

Kurt didn't try to reason with him. "It's no good, John. Won't work for me." Made no sense for him to explain his feelings. How could John relate to a man who felt like newly laid pavement that was blown away by the high winds ripping through Line Creek Canyon?

John moved on. "My winery colleagues don't know about any fieldwork right now. Timing is off, but if you can wait a few more weeks, I'll put a good word in for you at the Modesto Cooperative Winery. It's a growers' co-op only about two miles from here."

"Thanks. I appreciate your offer, in case," Kurt said. His hands sank deep into his pockets.

The next morning, Kurt rose early again to make coffee for him and John.

"I've thought about the orchard work some more," he said.

"No time to wait for the grapes to ripen. I'm going back to that big peach orchard, the one on Fairland, off Yosemite."

"I know the place," John said. He sipped his coffee and nodded absently in the early morning stillness.

∾

The day was already heating up when Kurt turned into the orchard a few minutes before eight. He pulled up next to a '53 Chevrolet, the same model that his mother drove all over eastern Oregon ranch country. From the looks of the thick film of dust and the grimy windows, it had taken a few back roads here in California.

By the time he turned off the motor, more cars and pickups had pulled into the dirt parking lot. He skipped the running board below the driver's door and planted both boots on the ground, the same pair of lace-up leather boots he'd worn everyday on the ranch. He counted on the thick, rubber soles to provide the balance he'd need in climbing tall ladders to reach the tops of fruit trees still laden with unpicked fruit.

He walked up to the small stucco house, painted white with emerald green trim around the two front windows. "This Land Is Your Land" blared from a radio inside. The weathered screen door slammed against the wood doorframe as workers walked in and out, flies buzzing around them.

A big, handwritten poster barely clung to the screen door with a torn strip of masking tape at the top. *"PICKERS SIGN IN HERE"* and in smaller letters below, *"LOS RECOGEDORES— POR FAVOR FIRMAR AQUI"*.

Kurt stared at the sign as men in jeans and fruit-stained T-shirts shuffled through the doorway. He reached in his shirt pocket for the pack of Pall Malls and lit up a cigarette. Okay, this was just temporary. He would find other work in a few days or weeks. John had said the wine co-op would need sugar level test-ers when the grapes were ready for harvest. That would involve some training. Better pay, too.

His mind kept reverting to fruit picking. Should he go with pay by the piece or by the hour? A quick calculation convinced him he'd earn more by the piece because he worked fast. He re-fused to think about it any longer, and grabbed the screen door as someone was coming out.

The manager stood inside the entry by the sign-up table. He recognized Kurt. "Good morning. Glover, right? So you decided this work might suit you after all?"

"Yes, sir. You said a man could get paid by the piece."

"Yep. Print your name, address, and social security number on the lined paper, clear enough so we can read it. We pay in cash at the end of every day, but we got to have correct records for the state labor people when they stop by."

Kurt leaned over the table, picked up the ballpoint pen, and started writing. He used John's home address. He put the pen down and looked up again. His new boss gave him clear instruc-tions.

"You'll find ladders and cardboard boxes in each orchard row. Grab a ladder and as many boxes as you might need for an hour or two. You have to keep track of your own boxes. Bring your full boxes back to the front parking lot here for inspection check-out."

Kurt nodded at the man. "Thanks. I'm all set."

As he shoved the screen door open, the sweltering heat hit him. It was hotter already than a July day in Wyoming. The ther-mometer hit a hundred and it wasn't noon yet. He tugged down on his straw cowboy hat to shade his face. That way, too, he didn't have to look into the eyes of the other workers. They were all here for the same reason.

He scanned the rows of trees to see which ones had the most

peaches ready for picking. Peaches hung in clusters just below the treetops, out-of-reach for most pickers. At six foot one, Kurt had a height advantage and longer arms than most. He grabbed the nearest wooden ladder and climbed several rungs.

He gradually established a rhythm. Spot the ripe peaches. Grab one, sometimes two, in each hand. Descend a few wobbly steps and plunk the peaches into the box below. He tried to pick fruit that was still firm to the touch. He kept flicking his face to clear away the peach fuzz that accumulated in his nostrils like loose feathers from an old down pillow. No time to use the cotton handkerchief in his shirt pocket.

Sweat poured down his face, coming to a point on his nose with the incessant drips. Sometimes he pinched the fleshy pulp too hard, or one would drop like a rock into the box below when his bulky work boot missed a rung of the shaky ladder. At day's end, those would cost him some of his hard-earned pay.

By the time he turned in his last box packed full of peaches that day, he was wiped out. It was the valley heat. The temperature reached one hundred seven that day. No escape, even in the shade of the fruit trees. His striped cotton shirt was wringing wet from sweat and his socks were soaked from the moisture trapped inside his boots.

He missed the summer afternoon thunderstorms that cooled things down on the high Wyoming plains. But he had grown more proficient at picking and packing the fruit. He could pack more into a box without damaging the fruit. More fruit in more boxes translated into more cash in his pocket.

He could do this job. He could last a few weeks until the co-op job came through. By then, David and Jean could come to live with them in Modesto. Not so sure about Linda. They hadn't talked to her since he took her to Ava's. Jo and he thought that she might as well stay there for the school year. Anyway, she now lived the life of Riley in southern California. She had her own bedroom for the first time, and a closet full of Francy's clothes.

He ground his last cigarette butt into the dirt with the tip of his boot before hopping into his pickup for the drive home. Coming home with some cash in his pocket brought a smile to his face.

19

THE ENGINE OVERHEATS

Kurt got used to driving his yellow and black, half-ton, GMC pickup to the orchard every day. The big chrome front grill still grabbed people's attention, but the routine didn't satisfy his appetite for longer drives in the country.

"Let's drive to Pinecrest tomorrow!" He grinned at Jo. "It's in the Sierra foothills. We can see some new territory."

"You're kidding! You can't afford to miss a day of work."

Jo was irked with him. The kids were scattered. She longed to move the family into a rental.

"This weekend, then."

She sighed. "Kurt, your enthusiasm always trumps my worries. You know that. But our living arrangement is wearing on me. Sometimes I want to scream, but of course I can't. The baby is crawling now, and we need to bring our big kids home. This can't go on!"

He hovered near her. "Come on! I know this is grating on you. I'm working harder than I ever have in those damned orchards. It's backbreaking work for a mere pittance. Glad that I'll be able to work for the winery soon. They'll train me how to conduct the sugar tests on the grapes soon as the harvest begins. And you'll get a secretarial job soon, too. Things will get better!"

He gave her a tight squeeze and felt her succumb to his wiles . . . for now.

"Let's talk John and Kathy into going with us this weekend.

We'll take all the kids. John says there's a beautiful lake where the kids can go swimming. Maybe you could try fishing again." He knew she had a soft spot for fishing in the mountains.

"Suppose so," she said.

Jo worried too much about things. A little outing would do her good. Pinecrest was eighty miles away. They would see new country and a river whose name he couldn't pronounce. "Too-all-oh-me," John slowly articulated. But after a try, Kurt returned to calling the Tuolumne River, "Two alumni". Other California place names suffered the same fate. San Jose became "San Josey" and Conejo was "Connie Joe". People found unexpected delight in his quirkiness. That inspired him to continue his folksy ways.

The weekend finally came. It was a beautiful day, not a cloud in the sky. Kurt relished the drive through the flat agricultural land of the Central Valley to the Sierra foothills. The hills transitioned gradually from scrub oak and digger pines to a much denser forest of towering sugar pines and giant sequoias. Taller and thicker, the trees were less rugged than in the Rockies, but the streams had the familiar willows and cottonwood trees on their banks.

As the two-lane highway took an increasingly twisting course, the engine sometimes lugged on the steep serpentine turns. Kurt throttled down to keep up the power. The outside air got cooler as they gained elevation, wafting through the open side windows. Suddenly, steam erupted from the hood. The rancid smell of heated oil from the engine suffused the cab.

"Damn it to hell! We've got to pull over. Looks like the engine's overheated." He honked the horn to get John's attention, but the Studebaker had already rounded the curve. "Don't worry, honey. We'll catch up with them. They'll figure out we had engine trouble."

Smoky puffs from the hissing engine filled the clean mountain air before Kurt found a suitable pullout along the narrow highway. "Better get out," he ordered Jo. He ran behind, pulled the tailgate to let the kids out, and grabbed the water jug tucked behind the bench seat.

"What's wrong?" the kids asked.

"The engine's too hot. You boys get back now. Don't want this steam to scald you!"

The engine hissed and steamed as he splashed it with water. He looked at Jo and the baby. "This is going to take a while. You'd better find a place to sit while the engine cools off."

She wedged her right foot into a horizontal crack of a huge granite boulder and pulled herself to the top with the baby in tow. The boys hung close by Kurt.

Kurt stomped around the truck, overheating himself like the engine. He'd made it all the way from Wyoming without any mishaps. No breakdowns. Not even a flat tire. Now this. Ruining a perfectly good day.

David and Jean were set to arrive on the Greyhound bus in three weeks, a day before school started. He thought about Linda, too. How he'd left her that Monday morning in late June with Ava and Charlie, relatives she barely knew.

They got to the park mid-afternoon. The wives set up their picnic amid the sequoias and pine trees. Sunlight dappled through the trees, warming parts of the sturdy oak picnic table.

Kurt stood nearby, silent in his thoughts. One of the boys perched on the empty picnic basket. The other begged his mother for another half-sandwich. Their younger sister grabbed onto the picnic bench, checking out the wood inch by inch. She was past the toddler stage though not like David or Jean, now ten and thirteen. It felt strange to be on an outing without them.

"Here's a sandwich for you," Jo said.

She looked pretty in her red pedal pushers and white, cotton, pullover shirt. Cropped shorter than usual, her thick, wavy hair was easier to manage. He wished he could make her life easier, too.

"Thanks." He pulled a cold beer from the Coleman chest and downed it between bites of sandwich.

In late August, John pulled Kurt aside one evening. "The grapes are ready for picking now. You should stop by Modesto Co-op Winery after work this week and see if they'll take you on. They're staffing up for the harvest. I called over there and talked to the manager, his name's Frank Alvarez. He said he could use a guy like you."

John explained the basic process of testing the sugar content of grapes to Kurt. "You'll have it down in no time. Main thing is you'll need to meet Frank and show him you're eager to do the work."

"You bet. Thanks, John."

"Job should last through October, maybe early November, if the winter rains hold off."

"Good. At least I won't have to pick and pack any more damned peaches."

And it would pay him enough to cover the bus trip for David and Jean to Modesto. Maybe even some of their school supplies.

Kurt drove to the co-op first thing the next morning. The winery plant sat on the right side of the highway just before the railroad tracks that marked the entrance to Empire—a town that shared the road traffic with its three, short blocks of commerce.

During the harvest season, a steady stream of trucks loaded with grapes stopped at the makeshift wooden platform where Kurt worked all day long. The tall platform was set up alongside the busy two-lane highway in front of the winery. He tested the grapes for sugar content before they were dumped onto large wooden pallets inside the grounds of the co-op. The growers were paid for their grapes based on sugar content and quality.

He grew adept at thrusting the big metal cylinder into the piles of grapes in the truck bed alongside the stand. He dropped a hydrometer inside the cylinder of crushed grapes to test the juice and read the measurement very loud so the grower could hear the results from inside his truck cab. High sugar content translated to higher price for the grapes.

It wasn't long before the growers recognized him when they pulled up to the platform. "Hey, Kurt," they would shout and greet him with a hearty wave. He liked the exchange. It reminded him of days on the ranch when he ran into the neighbors on his way into town.

School was about to start. He called his mother and asked her to arrange for David and Jean to take the Greyhound bus.

"I'll buy the tickets," she promised him.

"Thanks," he had said, grateful that he could keep his hard-earned cash.

David and Jean would soon be on their way. John and Kathy's house would get more crowded, but they'd figure out how to make it work. Linda would have to stay longer with Ava and Charlie. He wouldn't mind being spoiled like that for a little while himself.

20

REUNION AT THE GREYHOUND TERMINAL

Kurt glanced at his watch. 5:10 p.m. The bus was late.

A few people gathered outside the Greyhound terminal at 10th and G Streets. They paced the scorching sidewalk, stopping to listen when arrival announcements blared over the loudspeakers. The blocky sea-green tiles framing the lower front of the stucco building gave an illusion of coolness in the sweltering heat.

A young mother in a sleeveless cotton blouse, short-fitted skirt, and open-toed sandals, shared a cold bottle of Coke from the outdoor vending machine with her three young children. Two young Mexican day laborers, their faces and arms coated a burnished brown from too much sun, took stock of Kurt's tanned arms. They were a similar shade, a holdover from his ranching days in Wyoming.

The roar of the Greyhound bus startled him as it rounded the corner and slowed to make a left turn into the narrow driveway alongside the terminal. Kurt peered intently at the passing rows of windows to catch a glimpse of David and Jean, but the passengers formed a continuous blur through the windowpanes.

The big bus finally lurched to a stop in front of the side doors of the terminal. As soon as the door swung open, passengers flooded the crowded arrival area, fanning out in search of family members.

As more passengers stepped down from the bus onto the

shaded pavement, Kurt spotted them at last. Jean started down the steps first, dressed in a white T-shirt and faded blue jeans that looked a size too big. A sky blue, plastic headband pulled her shoulder-length, dark brown hair back from her chubby face. David, a step behind, looked over Jean's shoulder to find his father.

"Daddy!" Jean shouted.

"Dad!"

They raced to greet him.

David dragged the over-stuffed canvas duffel bag behind him with one arm and wrapped his other arm awkwardly around his father's waist. Jean was caught in between them.

"I missed you, Daddy," she said. She pressed her head into his chest.

"Ditto, honey." Kurt said, returning her hug before standing back to give them the once-over.

"Whoa. Looks like you've grown a couple of inches." He lightly tousled David's thick, dark brown, curly hair.

"You think so?" David said, fixing his eyes on his shoes.

"No doubt about it, Son."

"He hoped you'd notice," Jean spouted. She was as cute as ever. Big brown eyes and curly hair the same shade as her brother's. No change in her chubby cheeks and sturdy legs. She tugged at his shirt to get his attention.

"Daddy?"

"Yes?"

She glanced sideways at him.

"Where's Linda?"

"She's still in southern California with your great aunt and uncle."

"I thought she was supposed to come back by now."

"Yes, yes. She'll be back soon. Don't you worry about that. Besides, she's having a lot of fun living on that turkey ranch." He chuckled softly.

"You think so, Daddy? She told me how excited she is to meet Mr. George. He seems kind of crazy, with his bleached hair and purple robes and everything."

"Yep. He's a character."

"But she asked me when school starts here."

"She did?"

"Yeah. She's waiting for you to come get her."

"Well, that might not happen. Ava's got your sister enrolled in school down there now."

Jean braced her legs in front of him, fighting to stifle tears.

"Now, you'll see your sister soon enough. We have to rent a house first."

David fidgeted with the canvas handle of his duffel bag.

"Anyway, I miss her," Jean repeated, making sure they heard her.

"Yeah. Grandma got a little upset with Jean for crying for Linda so much. But I told her that Jean's used to having Linda around," David said.

David dragged his duffel bag closer to Kurt. "Can we get something to eat? I'm starving! Grandma fixed us a lunch that filled a grocery sack, but we ate most of it before the bus reached Reno."

"No kidding? You two are in a growth spurt. Luckily, your mother and Aunt Kathy are fixing dinner for us. Let's get going," Kurt said.

David stayed fixed in place. He wanted to share something with his dad first. "When Grandma put us on the bus this morning, there wasn't room for Jean and me, so the driver had us sit on the top step until we got to McDermitt."

"You did? That's a hundred miles! Did you notice the Steens? Beautiful country."

"Naw. We looked down the steps the whole way, through the big glass door. We watched pavement and sagebrush whizzing by. No mountains."

"Well, you made it okay, didn't you?" Kurt pressed his hands on David's back. "You guys will feel better when you have food in your stomachs. Put your gear into the back of the pickup."

David recognized the pickup. "There's Jimmy!"

He shared his dad's pride in having one of the first GMC pickups with automatic gears. When it was still new, David could drive around the ranch without having to reach for the clutch. It was an important invention for a kid who was barely five feet tall at the time.

Kurt pulled Jean onto the front seat from the passenger's side as David hopped up beside her and slammed the door shut. Kurt started the engine and they took off.

≈

A clutch of children ran from neighboring yards to greet them when they arrived at the house. Jean felt overdressed in her short-sleeve, plaid shirt, jeans and tennis shoes as she faced the barefoot crowd gathering around them. They all wore cotton T-shirts and summer shorts in bright colors.

Kurt caught sight of his oldest nephew and motioned to him. "Anthony! Come here, sonny boy. Meet your cousins!" The shy eight-year-old hung behind a couple of other boys, his T-shirt askew on his bony chest. He hesitated before forging a path through the kids. He glanced around Jean, unsure what to say, and looked up at David.

"Wanna help get our bags from Dad's pickup?" David asked, eager to get the pickup cleaned out.

"Sure," Anthony shrugged.

Kurt pointed at the duffel bags. "Put those in the carport for now. No room in the house for that kind of stuff."

But the sight of their mother rounding the corner distracted

Jean and David. Ignoring the intense summer heat and pesky flies buzzing around their faces, Jean dropped her bags and clutched her mother around her waist. David hovered behind them, the front of his shirt dripping with sweat. He tugged at his shirt to get fresh air inside before hugging his mother.

"My kids!" she said, drawing them tight. "You two must be starving. How does macaroni and cheese sound?"

"Good!" they shouted. They wriggled free of Jo's embrace and bounded for the front door.

"Hey!" Kurt hollered behind them. "You guys can't leave these bags out here."

They ran back, picked up the bags and stuffed them on a shelf in the carport before going inside to check out their new living quarters.

"Where am I going to sleep, Dad?" David asked. It was getting dark outside. "Aunt Kathy said Jean gets to sleep on the couch in the front room."

"The carport is your best bet, Son. Your uncle cleared his workbench for your sleeping bag, but he'll put down an old mattress on the floor if you want. I'll show you."

Floor-to-ceiling shelving in the back of the carport was jammed with boxes, Christmas decorations, and odds and ends. David brushed his hand across the cleared workbench.

"This'll be okay, Dad."

"Bully, boy."

Kurt knew David wouldn't mind sleeping out here. He could count on him. But he felt relieved anyway. The house was too crowded. Kids everywhere. Kurt sometimes wondered if he could stand another day of searching the house to find a pair of children's shoes, or swimsuits lost in a pile of dirty clothes that reached the top of the washer, or smelling the burnt toast because Jo forgot to raise the lever when there were so many other distractions in the kitchen. There was always a line for the bathroom. Even quiet space for reading the newspaper or opening the mail was at a premium. It got worse in the evenings when everyone was in the house at once.

~

Jo had enrolled Jean and David in the public schools near their neighborhood. El Vista Elementary was walking distance from John and Kathy's house on Glendale, but La Loma Junior High was over ten blocks away, far enough that most of the junior high kids rode their bikes to school.

The day before school started, Jean ran into Anthony showing David how to ride his old bike.

"Whose bike is that, David?" she asked.

"Anthony's."

"You can ride Benny's bike if you want," Anthony offered on his brother's behalf. But Benny objected. Jean wasn't surprised. He was a nervous boy, in fifth grade like her, who could be counted on to whine over just about anything.

"What's the matter here?" John asked, as he rounded the corner from the backyard.

"I don't want Jean riding my bike. Anyway, it's too big for her."

"I bet I can ride it as good as you, Benny."

"Let Jean use it, Benny."

Benny scowled at her before she got on.

"Thanks," she said. She didn't want them to know she'd never been on a bike before. She'd watched her brother practice. She swung her right leg over the crossbar and plunked herself onto the high seat. The bike teetered. She couldn't reach the pedals. She slipped down from the seat and captured the right pedal first, then the left, pressing down hard to get momentum. The bike lurched forward, wobbly at first.

"David! Anthony! Slow down!" she yelled at the boys who were down the block already. She'd meant to wave at Benny and John for letting her ride, but she didn't want to lose her grip.

21

THE REPLACEMENT DAUGHTER

It was late September and Linda still hadn't seen any sign of him.

"When is George supposed to come?" she asked her aunt one morning over breakfast. She slurped the milk from a cereal bowl of soggy Kellogg's Corn Flakes.

"This weekend. Don't expect to see him early Saturday morning, though. He likes to sleep in after being on the road so long."

"Goody," she said. She tipped her bowl to the side to get the last drops of milk.

"You need to use your spoon, dear, instead of slurping from your bowl."

Linda thrust the spoon into the bowl and plopped the bowl back on the table. She hated it when her aunt corrected her table manners. Ava didn't seem to understand people from Wyoming weren't country bumpkins. On their ranch, her parents had listened to BBC radio and debated with the neighbors about Adlai Stevenson and General Eisenhower when they campaigned for president last fall. Even at ten, Linda often joined her parents for the news broadcasts.

Linda wanted to ask if George ever stayed overnight in the luxurious ranch house on the other side of the alligator pen. But she couldn't get up the nerve. Ava referred to it as Betty's house, and Linda had never seen them together there. Ava said her sister Betty got the house after her divorce from George a few years before. Maybe Betty agreed that he could stay there the times when he returned from the wrestling circuit. After all, the house was on George's land, and Uncle Charlie managed the turkey operation for him. Or maybe, he just used it to store his stuff when he visited his ranch.

Two singsong bells rang out from the living room. Linda jumped to her feet and ran to the front door. Betty stood tall in her gold satin spiked heels and matching sheath dress that hugged her hips and bottom.

"Why, Linda. Good to see you this lovely morning. Where's your auntie?"

"She's in the carport with Charlie, showing him how to clean her car the right way."

"*She's* instructing *him*? That's amusing!"

"Do you want a drink of water or anything?" Linda knew her aunt would expect her to be hospitable.

"No thanks, dear."

Ava burst into the living room. "Betty! I heard the doorbell ring and figured it must be you."

The two sisters grasped each other's hands in mutual admiration. It was a familiar ritual.

"Why don't you kick off those spiked heels and relax for a minute on that cozy couch while I make us some iced tea?" Ava said. She pointed at the tapestry sofa in the alcove to the formal dining room.

"My favorite spot," Betty said.

Linda felt lucky to be included in this place designed for sharing sisterly secrets. She liked to sit cross-legged on the beige, shag carpet, her forearms resting on the glass coffee table across from the sofa. She could make a quick getaway if she got bored with their conversation.

Ava brought tall, frosty glasses of iced tea from the kitchen. She kicked aside her decorator sandals and curled her legs beneath her at one end of the sofa, ready to hear about Betty's latest adventures.

"Okay now! What's the news?" Ava said.

"George is back." That must mean he's visiting the ranch again, Linda thought.

"Oh, yes." Ava looked at Betty. "Linda's excited about meeting him."

"I've only seen him on TV," Linda added.

"You'll get the chance today, honey." She winked at her. "This ranch is his refuge from all that glamour stuff he does."

"No purple robe?"

"Heavens no! You'll see. He prefers white T-shirts and a pair of jeans when he's here. No reason for all that flamboyance around us."

Betty laughed. "The robe's his act. He loves to strut around the ring in a sequined robe, opening it to show off his muscular body. Sometimes people are aghast when he calls himself the 'Gorgeous One' or things like that, but it made him famous."

"He's quite the showman," Ava added.

"Yep. That goes back to the early 1940s when a lady at ringside yelled out, 'Isn't he gorgeous!' The crowed loved it and George added it to his next act."

"Matter of fact," she continued. "I gave him the idea of bleaching his dark brown hair and letting it grow out so he could curl it. Even though he won championship titles, he wasn't drawing big crowds to his wrestling matches until he played that 'gorgeous' card. I've pasted hundreds of sequins on those robes he wears!"

On a recent visit, Betty practically glowed when she talked about their marriage in the ring in Eugene, Oregon in 1939. "We were in the ring, surrounded by the cheering crowd. Afterwards, we decided to reenact the ceremony in wrestling arenas around the country. It was a smart move. We drew big crowds everywhere we went."

~

Later that afternoon, Linda, playing near the alligator pen, spotted George waving at her. A key dangled from a short chain attached to a gold bracelet on his wrist.

"Hey!" George said. "You must be Ava's niece." He flashed her a megawatt smile.

She hesitated, unsure what to say. He looked like Betty had described. Aside from his broad smile and the braided gold bracelet, he didn't look like a showman. No purple sequined robe. No Georgie pins or deep artificial waves in his platinum blonde hair. Instead, his bleached hair was slicked back into a ponytail at the base of his neck, exposing dark brown roots. His white T-shirt showed off his bulging arm muscles, and his well-washed Levis fit snugly to his thick waist. He was shorter than her father and a lot heavier.

"Are you going in there with the alligators?" she asked. An eight-foot-high chain link fence specially built for George's two pet alligators enclosed the pen.

"Yes, I have the key," he said, pointing to the key chain. "Do you want to join me?"

"I don't think so," she demurred. She was wary of the two gators lying like big slugs on the hot cement alongside a pool the size of a giant bathtub.

"Ah, come on. They won't bother you. It's hot today, and they're lazy critters. I bet I can't even get them to slip into the water."

"Okay," she said. She'd never seen them go into the pond.

"Follow me." He unlocked the gate and took the first step inside the pen. He grabbed a long, aluminum pole from the corner and extended it across the pool, landing it next to the alligator lolling there. The gator rolled his eyes up under his fleshy eyelids and slowly dragged his tail closer to the edge of the pool.

She and George stood back from the gators, watching them sun themselves. George kept tapping the concrete near the critters with the aluminum pole, trying to get their attention. At last, one gator budged. His big mouth, full of pointy teeth, gaped open. Linda stepped behind George and watched the gator crawl toward the pool's edge before slipping into the water. He settled briefly at the bottom of the pool, resembling a small submarine hiding from his visitors, before crawling up the other side to rest on the sizzling concrete slab.

"I guess that's all the action we're going to see today," George said. He motioned her through the gate and locked it behind them.

~

"Why does George have alligators?" she asked her aunt later that evening.

"They get people's attention," Ava replied. "Alligators are exotic animals. They add to George's mystique. And they draw visitors to the ranch. Turkeys are so ordinary, you know."

That made sense to Linda. When George had purchased the 195-acre ranch a few years before to raise turkeys, most of the turkey pens were located toward the back of the property, away from the entrance along Beaumont Road. Now, a few pens sat closer to the road. This gave visitors easy viewing access to the young turkeys dyed purple for show and the pen with the two alligators. People seemed to love the wacky scene. Visitors came to the ranch to see the purple turkeys and to get a glimpse of Gorgeous George.

One Saturday afternoon, Linda encountered a stocky, middle-aged woman staring at the baby turkeys with fluffy purple feathers.

"Are they born that way?" she asked.

"I guess so," Linda said matter-of-factly. She wouldn't give away George's secret of dunking the baby turkeys into a bucket of water with purple dye that made their fluffy feathers look like the iridescent purple flowers of an artichoke in full bloom.

It was all part of George's purple orchid theme at the ranch. The buildings were painted lavender to remind visitors of the "Human Orchid" they saw on his televised wrestling matches. Purple turkey burgers packaged in white boxes with purple orchids were sold in local grocery stores.

～

A few weeks later, a car screeched to a stop in the front driveway. The horn honked twice. It was George! She ran outside to greet him. It had been almost a month since she'd last seen him.

"Hey, Linda!" He smiled at her as he jumped out of his two-seater, red, Thunderbird convertible. He was duded up in a white shirt and metallic silver tie and dark gray slacks.

"Why aren't you out here playing tetherball with your girlfriends?"

"I was playing with them but they went home already."

"That's too bad. It's beautiful right now—a nice cool breeze."

An impish grin came over his face. "How about a lift over my head like I do the pro wrestlers in the ring?"

She gulped. "I'm not sure about that."

"Nothing to be afraid of!" He clutched her waist with both of his broad hands and lifted her high up. "Keep your body straight and I'll hold you like a platform over my head."

Her body stiffened. She didn't look down for fear of falling. She stayed stiff as a board as he braced her with his hands at the base of her neck and lower back. He lowered her gently to the ground.

"Good girl! Now you can tell your friends that Gorgeous George held you over his head, just like he does in the ring!"

"Whew!" she said, shaking her arms free. She stared at him so he wouldn't notice her trembling legs. She was proud that she hadn't shown him how scared she was, but she resolved never to let him lift her like that again.

"My brother David used to threaten me with a Charles Atlas move like that, but he couldn't lift me more than two inches off the ground."

"How old is he?"

"Twelve. No, he's thirteen now," she said proudly.

"He'll be able to do that one of these days. Especially if he takes up wrestling in high school, like I did."

"I won't let him get close enough to try it," she declared.

He chuckled and she smiled. She decided George wasn't trying to scare her. He was a big kid like David, only stronger.

❧

Linda had already started her sixth grade geography project on South America. She used Ava's Royal typewriter to type one-page descriptions of famous places like Iguazu Falls in Argentina and Sugar Loaf Mountain in Rio de Janeiro. She drew large, crayon drawings for each one, making a storybook about famous places in South America that she had first visited through the Encyclopedia that her parents had purchased, one book at a time. Now she depended on books checked out of her school library and a World Atlas that her aunt and uncle bought for her.

There were some things about school that Linda didn't bother to tell her aunt and uncle. Like how Mrs. Fisher told her she wanted to talk to them about having her skip sixth grade because she was so far ahead of her classmates. When Mrs. Fisher first mentioned it, she felt proud but wary. She would be a year younger than her new classmates.

"True," Mrs. Fisher said. "But think about the advantages. You'll be with students who are more advanced like you. You can change classrooms every hour and add a music or PE course to your schedule."

Linda wasn't convinced.

"Okay then. I'll talk to your aunt and uncle about it, but we won't make any rash decisions. Let's see how it goes this fall," Mrs. Fisher said.

"Thanks," she said. Maybe Mrs. Fisher would forget about it. Anyway, she hoped her father would pick her up soon and take her home to Modesto. She kept thinking what it would be like to go to school with Jean again. Though her little sis was a pest sometimes and jabbered a lot, Linda missed her. David, too.

Charlie and Ava were always on the go. Although he stuck close to home, Charlie worked hard on the turkey operation. He had a steady stream of visitors to the house, like the man who sold him feed for the turkeys and the freelance photographer who came by to photograph the purple turkeys for promotion at George's wrestling events.

During the week, Ava often had people from her church over for the evening, and sometimes on Saturdays she went around neighborhoods with church couples to distribute religious pamphlets. It wasn't the kind of church Linda was used to. Ava called it a Kingdom Hall for Jehovah's Witnesses. Luckily, Ava didn't seem to mind that Linda stayed at home playing records or doing her homework when they went to church.

Despite their busy schedules, Charlie and Ava helped Linda with her homework at night and attended parent-teacher conferences held at the elementary school that fall.

At the second conference in late October, a few days before Halloween, Mrs. Fisher laid out Linda's homework assignments and tests on a long foldout table for viewing by Ava and Charlie. Linda pulled up a well-used oak chair to Charlie's right at the end of the table.

After scanning the papers, Ava exclaimed, "Isn't this terrific, Charlie? Her marks are all A's, even an A+ for work on her geography project." Her teacher had added a comment to the A+, *"Best I've ever seen in sixth grade."*

Ava leaned forward over the table to catch a glimpse of Linda who was busily drawing little stick figures on a piece of lined paper. "We're so proud of you honey! Your work reminds me of Francy's. She was a top-notch student like you."

Ava's mention of Francy made her uneasy. They always talked about her outdoor activities, not her schoolwork, like how much she liked to swim or go hiking in the San Jacinto Mountains. Linda squirmed in her chair. "It's not so hard. I like the classes, especially math and English." She felt embarrassed by their praise. Her parents always expected her to get good grades, and if David and Jean were here, they'd razz her about all the attention she was getting.

~

Almost two months had passed since her father had dropped her off at Ava and Charlie's place. She was used to the weekday routines of attending school, playing tetherball at home afterward with her friends, and doing homework after watching American Bandstand on TV before dinner. Every Friday night, Ava and Charlie treated her to a burger basket with a pile of French fries and a delicious chocolate shake. It was her favorite meal.

Now that fall was setting in, and the evenings were getting cooler, she found herself thinking about her family in Modesto more often. As she sat on her bed one evening, listening to "Sixteen Tons" by Tennessee Ernie Ford on Francy's record player, she started snapping her fingers and singing along,

"Some people say a man is made out of mud. A poor man's made out of muscle and blood. Muscle and blood and skin and bones, a mind that's weak and a back that's strong. You load sixteen tons and what do you get? Another day older and deeper in debt."

She stopped singing in the middle of the song. She had sung that tune so many times on the radio in Wyoming. But now it made her think about her dad. How hard he had worked on the ranch. She remembered how he had tried to cultivate the rock-strewn fields across the river from their house. It was tough for him to dig a fence posthole into the hardpan. He broke his shovel once while trying to repair a fence.

She hadn't heard from her parents since her father left her with Ava and Charlie. Thanksgiving was only a month away. Maybe he was having a hard time finding a job that didn't require a college degree like Uncle John had. And he wasn't like George who could use his showmanship to promote himself at televised wrestling spectacles around the country.

Her mother must have a secretarial job by now. They were probably still living with John and Kathy and their kids on Glendale Avenue. But it must be extra crowded with David and Jean living there, too. She stopped herself. They must be back by now from her grandparents' ranch.

She tried to remember Christopher's sweet baby smells. She wanted to touch him and hear his coos. And she wondered how

Jean did in her new school without David. It was the first time the three of them hadn't gone to the same school together.

~

"Put on a dress, dear, and then put this box of pamphlets in the backseat of the car. We're going to the worship services at the Kingdom Hall."

It was Sunday again. She'd grown used to staying at home Sunday mornings. When her aunt and uncle got back from church, they always brought her leftover doughnuts in a covered cardboard box.

"What do you mean?" Linda asked. Why did she need to put on a dress?

"It's silly for you to stay here alone every Sunday morning. We want you to go with us."

She hadn't expected it. Her aunt knew she'd gone to the Catholic Church with her family. They saw Our Lady of the Valley Church when they had visited the Wyoming ranch.

"Can't I stay here, Auntie?"

Ava refused. "No. We want you with us." She pursed her thick, red lips. "You'll like the service. People sing and pray and do some readings from the Bible. Everyone is friendly."

Linda wasn't worried about people being nice to her. She wasn't sure if it would be a mortal sin or not, but she was positive no one from her family had ever gone to a Kingdom Hall. "Can you call Mom and Dad to see if it's okay with them?"

Ava looked at her as if she'd grown a second set of arms and legs. "My goodness, Linda. What a question! Your parents will be thrilled that you're going to church with us. They won't think twice about it."

She could tell that Ava didn't want her parents to know. Auntie wasn't being on the up-and-up with them. This made her feel queasy. What if her parent's got mad when they found out? What if God got mad?

"Maybe after we go to church, we can plan our trip to Hollywood," Ava said. "Would you like that?"

"Yes, Auntie," she blinked in surprise. Ava and Charlie liked to spoil her. A few weeks ago, Auntie had promised they would take her on a trip to Hollywood during the winter school break. She had jumped with excitement over the idea of seeing a big movie studio. It almost felt like she was their daughter. But she wasn't.

She missed her family. If only they weren't so far away. She thought about Francy, too, how she liked to take risks. *She* would have gone to the Hall with her parents. As much as Linda thought it might be a sin, she wondered, what harm would it do? Especially since they would take her to Hollywood soon. Besides, she reasoned, it was a good way to thank them for taking care of her. She was just being gracious. Nothing wrong with that.

She strode to the passenger side of the car, shoved the box filled with religious pamphlets onto the backseat, and ran into the house to put on a dress. Hollywood was the only thing on her mind.

~

The meeting hall was plainer than she expected. There were rows of folding chairs facing a speaker's podium and doughnuts and punch in the reception hall. The rows of windows on either wall were regular glass, and there weren't any statues of Jesus and Mary. The Witnesses smiled at her and made a point of talking with her after the service.

By the time she arrived home, Linda was worn out. She thought about Ava's promise to take her to Hollywood. Was it worth it? A few more weeks and she'd get to go. Her dream was in sight. Anyway, going to the meeting hall wasn't as terrible as she'd feared. The people weren't mean to her or anything. It's just that it wasn't Catholic. She missed the familiar Latin chants of the Mass, the genuflections, and being able to walk to the rail with her family for Communion.

Would her father and her grandmother be upset with her? When they lived in eastern Oregon, many Sundays she went to Mass with her grandmother and her family at St. Bernard's. Generations ago, family names had been etched in the stained glass windows of the old Catholic Church built with blocky granite stones. Her grandmother would shout out the hymn number before playing the creaky organ. Oftentimes, other family members and neighbors slipped into the pews a few minutes late, passing right by her grandmother seated at the organ, but Grandma never let on that it bothered her.

She had knelt alongside her grandmother many times to say the rosary before Mass. She could hear her grandmother's sing-song voice as she fingered each bead, *"Hail Mary, full of grace. The Lord is with thee . . ."* She would stand next to her when she played the organ during Mass. The numbered songs from the hymnal were listed in chalk on the small, square blackboard sitting on a rickety easel placed next to the altar so everyone could see.

~

By Thanksgiving, she had attended several services at the Kingdom Hall. Although always uneasy when they left the house, once she arrived, Linda had a good time with the families and sometimes got to play outside with the kids afterward. When they walked door-to-door through neighborhoods of Beaumont on Saturday mornings to deliver Watchtowers and Awakes, she got to know the kids better, too. Ava had arranged for her to go with them, but Linda stayed behind as they walked up to the door and knocked.

"You're pretty shy, aren't you?" one or the other would say in her defense.

"Guess so," she'd reply.

≈

One Sunday, as she helped Mrs. Rustan put away the folding tables, Mrs. Rustan asked about her family. Linda gave the usual explanation. "They're living with my aunt and uncle in Modesto until they find a house to rent. It's pretty crowded with all the kids."

"I bet you miss them a lot. And they must miss you, too." At that moment, it felt like Mrs. Rustan was her second mother. Linda wanted to talk to her about it some more but she hardly knew her.

Mrs. Rustan leaned close. "Your great aunt and uncle are lucky to have you. Francy's fall last year was so tragic. They were devastated. You're a bright light for them."

Linda beamed. That confirmed what she'd hoped: that going to church with Ava and Charlie helped them feel a little better after losing Francy. But she started thinking about her family. She hadn't heard from them in months. Could they have given her away?

The thought startled her. It brought back David's warning at her Grandma's house. She was certain he was dead wrong, but now she wondered if maybe her parents had agreed to let Ava and Charlie adopt her like they had adopted Francy and Sandra. After all, Francy was dead, and Sandra had moved away from home when she got married a few years ago.

She gradually talked herself out of the awful notion. Her parents wouldn't give her up. She remembered her dad's promise, "This is only temporary. We'll bring you back as soon as we get a home."

No matter. She didn't want to be Ava and Charlie's daughter. Christmas was coming up. She longed to hear from her family. Long distance was expensive, and the Modesto house was probably too noisy to make phone calls. Even a short call would be good since Ava said that Jehovah's Witnesses didn't celebrate Christmas.

22

THE LUMP

On a November morning, Kurt waited for Jo to get out of the bathroom. She usually showered and dressed for work quickly, but she was still in the bathroom at seven forty. He rapped on the door.

"Jo!"

The door swung open. She stood there, still dressed in her slip and nylons, her face pale as her white slip.

"Something the matter? You're running late," he said.

"There's a lump on my neck."

"What?"

"Here, take a look. I can't see it in the mirror unless I hold my head straight back like this." Her hair touched her shoulders as she arched her neck back.

He moved in close to check it out. "There's something there, all right. It's red and swollen. Have you noticed it before?"

"A few weeks ago."

"You haven't mentioned it."

"I hoped it would go away. Now it's starting to worry me."

"You better see a doctor."

"You know we don't have a doctor here yet, and I won't have health insurance for another five months." The law firm required six months employment first.

"Better go anyway. We'll figure out a way to pay."

"I suppose." She looked at her watch. "I've got to finish getting dressed."

He watched as she applied extra face powder to her neck before pulling her dress over her head. She buttoned the four top buttons and cinched her narrow belt to her waist. It closed easily at the third notch—a sign that she was losing weight. He often teased her about how slender she was. "Turn sideways so I can see your shadow," he'd say. And she'd laugh. But now she looked too thin. Unlikely Jo'd make an appointment for herself, but Kathy would know a good doctor. He'd ask her when they got home that evening.

~

A couple of days later, he handed Jo a scrap of paper with the address of a Dr. Williams. "Kathy got you an appointment with a doctor to check that lump."

Jo studied the paper. "That was nice of her." The appointment was set for the following Thursday morning at nine o'clock, a week before Thanksgiving.

"We can stop by on our way to work. I'll drop you off afterwards. You might be a few minutes late, but not much more, then I'll head to the wine co-op."

"My boss won't mind," she said, shrugging her shoulders.

He could tell she was skittish about it. "Hey, Jo. We need to find out what we're dealing with here."

"I know"," she said absently. "But don't say anything to the kids."

"'Course not. No need to worry them."

~

When Kurt drove up to the medical office building that Thursday morning, he could barely make out the building through the tule fog. John had warned him about the dense valley fog that causes lots of traffic accidents every winter. As they walked together to the front door, Jo wrapped her black and white tweed coat snugly around herself to ward off the chill.

"I'll stick around while you see the doc," he said, lightly brushing his hand under her chin to get her attention.

She turned away. "Good. I just want to get this over with." Her voice dropped as low as the foggy air hovering over the ground.

~

They waited a few minutes in the waiting room. The white walls and matching baseboards sharply contrasted with the colorful purple chambray chairs and mahogany end tables. Magazines, fanned out for visitors, caught Kurt's eye and he picked up an old *Readers Digest*.

At last, the nurse called Jo into the exam room. Everything was institutional white, including the sideboard, making the precisely arranged steel exam tools stand out. Kurt sat forward on the visitor's chair, planting his hands firmly on his knees.

"This'll be over with before you know it," he announced.

"Hope so," was all he could coax out of her.

Dr. Williams entered the room wearing the standard white coat and a warm smile designed to make her feel more at ease. After brief pleasantries, he quickly got down to business.

"So you've discovered a lump on your neck? When did you first notice it?"

"A few weeks ago."

"Let me take a look." He inspected her neck.

"How long has it looked like this Mrs. Glover?"

"It was the size of a small pebble when I first noticed it, but it's gotten bigger."

"Have you experienced any pain?"

"No."

"She didn't even tell me until a few days ago," Kurt said.

The doctor nodded at him. He pressed his middle fingers against her neck again and stroked up and down.

"Can you feel the lump when I press here?"

"Yes."

Dr. Williams pulled his hands away from her face and wheeled his chair back from the exam table.

"Mrs. Glover, this is what we're going to do. I want to put you in the hospital as soon as possible so we can remove that lump and relieve the pressure on the artery in your neck."

"I can't afford to miss any work."

"Well, you may have to miss a day or two. We also need to determine whether the growth is malignant or not."

Her chest heaved assent.

～

The procedure went smoothly. Kurt and Kathy were by Jo's bedside when she came out of the anesthesia late in the afternoon.

"What's the word?" she asked.

"We don't know anything yet. The doctor said he'll have the lab report in a day or two."

Dr. Williams called her later in the week. It was Hodgkin's, a cancer of the lymph system. "We can treat it with a combination of chemotherapy and radiation." The chemo was experimental, he explained. A form of mustard gas that was used in World War I. "This is a much weaker dosage, and we think it will be effective against the spread of the cancer into the lymph nodes. I'm using it on another patient with the same type of cancer you have."

Jo trembled at the news. They set her first chemo treatment

for the following Monday.

~

At the hospital, the nurse prepped her on the exam table before giving her a shot in the right hip. "This'll help with the pain," the nurse said.

"Do you always give a shot like this?" Jo winced from the jab.

"No. This is just extra precaution because the drug is new for this use."

Jo glanced up at Kurt for reassurance. "I feel woozy. Like I might throw up." She shuffled off the table to the linoleum floor. "Where's the bathroom?"

"Down the hall, to your right," the nurse said.

Kurt took her arm as she walked. "Now, honey. You're going to be okay. We can go home soon." But he was alarmed by how frightened she was. From outside the bathroom, he could hear her dry heaving. She finally emerged, her face drained, her hands trembling. He suddenly felt alone. What if the treatment failed? This was a first for both of them. They'd get through this, but it would take some time, and maybe a small miracle. His head drooped at the thought.

A different nurse came in a short time later and stuck a large needle into the vein in Jo's right arm for the intravenous intake of the mustard gas. The large tube dripped liquid into her vein for hours. But Jo wasn't tracking the time.

She vomited all night long and couldn't control the diarrhea that soaked the sheets. "I'm so embarrassed," she whispered to Kurt, her arms hanging limply by her side.

"Jo's sick as a dog," Kurt reported to Kathy later that evening. "The doctor said she can go home 'soon as she recovers from the treatment, but she's going to need some help."

"I'll help take care of her," Kathy offered.

He barely looked up, afraid to show his deep fear about Jo. "Appreciate it."

~

By early December, Jo was back at work. "I don't have sick leave, and I can't miss any more work," she had insisted. "We've got to have the income."

Still, she felt incredibly weak. That was the hardest part. Her boss expected her to type legal documents and business correspondence all day long. By five o'clock, she left the office exhausted. But she was grateful that the kids weren't aware of her illness. Only David had asked her why she was going to bed so early.

"Long days at work," she replied. Thank goodness he accepted that explanation. Thank goodness, too, that she hadn't lost her hair from the chemo treatments. The only noticeable effect was her weight loss. Her clothes now hung on her.

Shortly before Christmas, Dr. Williams assured her she wouldn't have to endure any more chemo treatments because the mustard gas seemed to be working. But he wanted her to begin radiation treatments in January after the holidays.

"We want you to enjoy the holidays, Mrs. Glover. I hope you'll eat lots of ham and mashed potatoes so you gain some of that weight back."

She smiled wanly at him. "Food is the farthest thing from my mind."

~

A new Pacific storm came through every few days, pounding the streets with rain that filled the gutters and caused low-lying areas to be flooded. This continued until the rain subsided and the storm sewers could absorb the extra water.

One rainy morning, David took off for school on his bike, leaving Jean to ride alone. When she approached the main intersection with the traffic lights, Jean noticed a policeman flagging cars to slow them as they drove through the flooded intersection. She kept to the side of the pavement to avoid the flooded area and ducked her head low to fend off the rain.

As she left the intersection and entered the next block, she saw David's crushed bike fallen sideways alongside the road. Her brother, a few feet away, squirmed in pain. She dropped her bike to the narrow shoulder of the road and raced to him.

"What happened?" She knelt by him, sticking her knee into the muddy bank to steady herself.

"A car hit my bike. My leg hurts pretty bad," he said. Clad in soaked jeans, his right pant leg ripped through above his knees. His exposed thigh looked like fresh hamburger meat.

"You mean the driver didn't stop to help you?"

"No. Guess he didn't see me fall."

"I'll get that policeman to help you. Then I'll run back home. Dad should be there still." Her father's job at the winery co-op had ended in November with the start of the rainy season.

The policeman called for an ambulance and promised to wait there with David.

~

"Your leg is pretty banged up," the doctor said. "But I don't see a major fracture. I'll clean up the wound on his thigh."

Kurt watched as the doctor worked on David's leg. Every so often Kurt looked over at David to see how he was doing. He hadn't said a word during the procedure. The silence between them felt electric.

"What happened, Jean? Were you there?" Kurt asked.

She told him how she found him sprawled alongside the road next to his smashed bike. "He had mud all over him!"

"Good girl to help your brother. You guys have got to quit riding on that road. It's too dangerous for bikes."

"Do you think Anthony will be mad at me for wrecking his bike?" David asked.

"'Course not. And we'll get someone to fix it."

Jean rolled up her eyes at David. They knew their father was better at finding a repairman than fixing something himself.

～

With seven children in the house, preparations for Christmas soon consumed everyone. Jo convalesced from the chemo treatments, so Kurt took it upon himself to carry forward their Christmas Eve tradition.

He loved playing Santa Claus and had never missed a year in this role, even when they lived at Badger Basin. When he discovered his Santa outfit hadn't made it to California, John came to the rescue.

"I'll bet we can borrow one from the school."

Kurt patted his brother-in-law on the back. He could barely contain his excitement.

On Christmas Eve, after a big spaghetti feed, Kathy did the dishes and cleaned the kitchen while Jo rested. John followed Kurt into the carport to help him put on his Santa outfit. The big kids—David, Anthony, and Jean—were out there, too. They had pleaded with Kurt to let them act as Santa's assistants. He agreed but swore them to secrecy about keeping Santa's identity from John and Kathy's three other young children.

They helped Kurt tape the fluffy white beard above his sideburns and carefully pulled the Santa hat over his ears to cover his thick head of black hair. As Jean filled a large white pillowcase with presents for the kids, the boys helped Kurt stuff two pillows inside his baggy pants to fill them out. For the finishing touch, David pulled the big, black belt out of the costume box and cinched his father's bulging waist. Kurt transformed into a jolly, rotund Santa.

They waited for their mothers to signal that the children were ready for Santa's arrival. At last, they heard the knock on the door from the kitchen.

David handed him a cluster of small bells that he could ring when he stopped at each window and peered inside to shout "Ho! Ho! Ho!" at the astonished children. Crammed with Christmas gifts, the white pillowcase was slung over his shoulder. Santa had enough presents to give one gift to each child.

Kurt appeared at each window, cupping his hand and waving at the children inside. As he progressed from window to window, the kids got more excited. They shrieked in delight.

When he completed a full circle of the house, Kurt knocked at the front door and again shouted "Ho! Ho! Ho!" in his deep and familiar voice.

The younger kids hid behind their mothers' legs, peeking around to get a glimpse of Santa. Only Benny stepped forward to check him out from head to foot. He stopped abruptly when he recognized Kurt's work boots. "Hey! You're not Santa," he said. "Those are Uncle Kurt's boots!"

"Look, Benny," Jean said. "I think you'd better apologize to Santa. He came all the way from the North Pole just to bring us presents, didn't you, Santa?"

"Yes!" Santa replied. He dropped his bag of presents to the floor and reached inside for gifts. "Why here's a present just for you, Benny!" Benny clutched his present and grinned up at Santa.

After he emptied the pillowcase, Santa left. Later, Jean spotted her father down the hall as she walked into the living room to make up the sofa bed.

"Daddy, are we going to call Linda for Christmas?"

"Tomorrow, honey. You need to get some sleep now."

～

On Christmas day, Kurt dialed Ava and Charlie's phone number. "Hello, Ava. Kurt here. Merry Christmas to you and Charlie. Is Linda there?"

"Linda!" his voice boomed as if he were calling long distance on a party line. "It's Dad. Merry Christmas!"

She could hear Jean say something to her father.

"Jean's sitting here next to me. Are you having a good Christmas, honey?"

"Pretty good. Ava fixed a nice dinner today, but there weren't any Christmas presents." She wasn't sure if her father knew about Jehovah's Witnesses and holidays. "Ava and Charlie don't celebrate Christmas. They're Jehovah's Witnesses."

The phone line was silent. Linda's comment jolted Kurt. Out of nowhere, his memory clicked and he remembered how Ava had said something to him about how she and Charlie had become Jehovah's Witnesses after Francy's death. That was when he dropped off Linda last August. He guessed it was their way of finding solace from their grief. He had told Jo about it later, but they agreed they didn't know much about that religion.

"Dad?"

"Yes, honey?"

"Did you and Mom send me a Christmas present?"

"I think so. Hasn't it got there yet?"

"Not yet," she said.

"It'll be there soon, honey. Why don't you ask your mother? She's right here waiting to talk to you. Your sister and brother are pounding on me, too."

Linda's voice cracked. "Merry Christmas, Mom. I miss you!"

"We miss you too. I'll get a gift off to you tomorrow."

Linda flinched. Her father hadn't told her the truth. Why? He must feel bad about forgetting to send her a Christmas present in time.

Jo continued, "I've been kinda sick the past few days."

"Oh. Hope you're feeling better."

Jo tried to sound chirpier. "Yes, I'm getting better every day."

"That's good, Mom."

"You would have enjoyed seeing your dad play Santa again this year. He had to borrow a Santa suit from the elementary school. It was too big for him. He had to stuff two pillows into the pants!"

Linda laughed. "Were the little kids scared of him?"

"At first. But they warmed up when he started handing out presents."

Linda talked with David and Jean. Mostly, David would tell a joke and the girls would laugh, like always, but Linda felt like crying instead.

Kurt interrupted them. "Listen, honey. We've got to end this call. Long distance is so damned expensive."

"Dad. Before you hang up. Are you going to get a house soon?"

"Hope to start looking in January, or maybe February. We'll let you know."

It felt as if somebody had smashed her against the wall. Oxygen escaped her lungs and taking a breath seemed impossible.

"Linda? Are you there?"

"Yes, Dad." She choked up. "Can I say goodbye to Mom, David, and Jean?"

"Okay. But you'd better make it quick. Bye-bye, now."

∾

By two-thirty, the call was over. Kurt turned to Jo, "How'd she sound to you?"

"Lonely."

"Now, honey. She'll be fine. It's just hard at Christmas."

"I guess so," she said, untying her apron. "I think I'll take a nap now." He'd never seen her look so defeated.

23

BAPTISM IN YANKEE STADIUM

Ava peered into Linda's bedroom. "Linda?"

"Yes?" She kept stacking the forty-five records in neat piles on the carpet, not looking up.

Ava shifted from one foot to the other in the doorway, biding her time before making the announcement. "Charlie and I are treating you to a special trip to New York City this summer—in July, after school is out. We're going to see the Empire State Building and Yankee Stadium." She beamed down at Linda, waiting for her response.

Linda twisted around. "Really! You mean fly there? I've never flown in a plane before, you know!" Her hand glanced off the stack of records in her excitement, spilling them onto the carpet.

"Your records!" Ava said.

Linda steadied herself. "I'll fix them in a minute. You mean we're going in June, not July, right?"

"No, in July. We'll fly from LA to New York—takes about six hours. We'll stay at a hotel in Manhattan. It's a perfect place for seeing the sights and going shopping."

Linda squirmed. "But, Auntie. Daddy's coming to get me in June."

"Well, he's got a temporary job now and can't come down until later this summer. Not sure exactly when."

Linda gulped. "When did you talk with him?"

"Sunday night. You were already asleep when we reached him."

"And he didn't mind?" She looked at her aunt for signs that maybe he did mind. Maybe Ava just didn't want her to know.

"Mind what, dear?"

"Mind not picking me up until July?"

"Oh. He was disappointed. That's for sure. But he was excited that you'd have a chance to fly to New York City with us. First time, and everything."

"Oh," she sighed, fighting back tears. She felt stranded on this island, this big, fat, rich place without any of her real family around. Her father must know how excited she was about coming home as soon as the school year ended. He'd left her here last August, almost ten months ago. Worse still, he'd promised her.

She looked around to find something familiar: the picture of Christopher in the Webers' living room in Badger Basin when he came home from the hospital; the army blanket she brought with her to Beaumont. Her parents had called her only once, at Christmas, since she had started school last fall. She figured it was because they couldn't afford long distance. But now, she wondered, maybe they don't care. They would have called her if they cared. Maybe they had forgotten her in all their troubles. Too many other problems to solve. Another temporary job meant her father was still getting on his feet.

She remembered how they would run outside their Wyoming ranch house to answer the phone when they heard the honk of the car horn. Sometimes they didn't get there in time. The phone was hooked up to the horn inside the car. But here in California, there was a phone on the kitchen wall and one in the living room. Her parents could reach her easily if they wanted. More than once a year, for sure. Had they forgotten how she had helped out the family when they lived in Badger Basin? It was hard times there, too, but they stuck together.

Her aunt always gave the same explanation. "Your folks are busy getting settled in a new city, dear. They haven't forgotten you."

Ava didn't blink this time either.

"He thinks you'll have a wonderful time. It'll only be a short delay before you can go home with him."

Linda shivered. "I know. But it makes me sad anyway!" It didn't made sense to her. Why couldn't her aunt tell she was upset? She started pulling the paper slipcovers off her records and spreading them around the floor.

Ava swung her arms through the air as if waving a magic wand to wipe away Linda's disappointment. "Now, dear. Don't fret about this! Anyhow, we won't be going anywhere unless you finish your sixth grade project this month. How are you doing on that?"

"I only have to finish the drawing of Sugarloaf Mountain in Rio de Janeiro." It was for the cover to her book on South America.

Linda's thoughts reverted to the airplane trip. David and Jean were sure to be amazed.

"Do you suppose David and Jean could go with us?"

"What?" Ava said. She looked surprised. Her eyelashes, thick with black mascara, wouldn't stop blinking.

"How sweet of you to think of them! But that won't be possible. Maybe another time." She patted Linda on the shoulder and left the room.

Linda fell back upon her bed, sinking into the puffy comforter. She buried her head in the feather pillow. It was no use arguing with her aunt, and Charlie would just reassure her that this was a great thing to do. But she desperately missed her family. She had pictured her father driving up the circular driveway to take her home after the school year was over in June. She had imagined her arrival at their new house many times. Hugging her mother. Seeing David and Jean again. They'd probably tease her about her nice clothes. And the baby! She couldn't imagine how he might have changed. Could he walk now? Would he remember her? Excitement and trepidation filled her simultaneously.

She must have fallen asleep. She was awakened by her aunt's call to dinner. Her pillowcase felt damp from her tears.

"I'm not hungry, Auntie," she said. Her body quivered.

"I'm sorry to hear that, dear. Please join us at the table, anyway."

❧

The flight to New York City was longer than she expected. They left Los Angeles about six-thirty Friday morning. As the plane soared into the sky, Linda gripped the seat arms. The buildings below grew smaller by the second. When the pilot announced they were making a big loop over the Pacific before heading east, she gasped in wonder.

"We're flying over the ocean?"

The plane pierced the clouds, engines full-throttle as it gained speed and altitude. She sank deeper into her seat and pulled the blanket over her lap. It felt good to have something warm and comfy over her. She stuck her nose on the window and skewed her eyes downward to get a better view of the distant landscape below.

As the plane droned on, she took advantage of every food cart that came down the aisle. When the pilot announced their descent into the New York City area, she had already devoured two meals and accepted every bottle of Coca-Cola and bag of salty peanuts the stewardess offered her.

❧

Ava had booked a room in the Hilton on West 53rd, a few blocks from Central Park. When the cab driver dropped them off in front of the hotel, Linda felt dwarfed by the building. She scrunched her neck to see the top.

"You have to back away to see the top of the building." Charlie guided her across the street where they could see the hotel and other brick buildings stretched like a single massive wall to the next intersection. The buildings blocked the sunlight and cast long shadows on the sea of people walking on the sidewalk below. Only the colorful changing lights at the intersection and the headlights of yellow cabs added sparkle and life to the immense brick fronts.

Inside the Hilton, Linda wandered around the bustling lobby as Ava and Charlie checked in. Fixated on the busboys hauling piles of luggage on brass-plated carts with wheels, excitement suddenly roared through her. New York City! Wait until David and Jean hear about this. She couldn't wait to explore. She scanned the opulent room. The elevators opened and a large group of passengers filed out. The bell captain's plastered smile greeted guests with questions. The entry. How many people stayed here? The revolving entry door barely had a chance to stop. A gigantic poster. A welcome sign. A woman in a bright blue dress. Wait! Shot her eyes back to the welcome sign and read it. It felt as if her heart dropped, her excitement fizzled, and her stomach twisted.

"Jehovah's Witnesses: Welcome to the New York Hilton. We hope you enjoy your stay in New York City."

Framed just below the welcome message, a poster with a black and white photograph of Witnesses at the 1957 convention at Yankee Stadium was highlighted. The stadium was full of people. Even the baseball diamond was invisible. But she recognized the dugouts on either side of the field.

She stared at the poster and the photograph, trying to absorb what this meant for her visit to New York City. She was jolted by the memory of people in the Jehovah's Witnesses Hall in Beaumont talking about a convention in New York City. If Ava and Charlie had plans to take her to the convention, they hadn't mentioned it.

After the busboy left their hotel room, Linda finally had a chance to ask them about the convention.

"Did you see the big poster about a Jehovah's Witnesses convention here?"

"Why, yes," Charlie said. "They hold the convention here every year. Witnesses come from all over the world. You haven't heard mention of it at the meeting hall?"

"I guess so." She brushed him off.

Ava grabbed her hand and pulled her to the sofa. "We wanted to surprise you. It's such a special opportunity. There will be thousands of Witnesses there, just like us."

"But I'm not a—" she started to say.

"That's true," Charlie interrupted. "You aren't a Witness yet. But you can attend with us."

She felt nervous over what he said. *Yet?* "At Yankee Stadium?" she asked.

"Yes. The same place where the Yankees play the Red Sox. The Witnesses have reserved it for a whole week. One hundred thousand people attended the assembly last year! In fact, they expect so many people they've booked the Polo Grounds too. It's across the river from Yankee Stadium."

"Does Daddy know?"

"No, dear. There's no point in telling him. He doesn't understand what being a Witness is about. Not like you do. You are a very special girl in Jehovah's eyes."

"Daddy probably doesn't know anything about conventions because Catholics don't have them." Worst of all, he'd be furious with her if he found out she was going to a Jehovah's Witness convention. He'd be mortified to learn that she had participated in a non-Catholic church event. He would expect her, like all his children, to practice the Glover family's faith. It was how he'd been raised, and how he had raised her.

She felt squished inside a box without enough air. Only the thought of David and Jean lightened her mood, though they wouldn't believe she had come all the way to Yankee Stadium for a church convention instead of going to a baseball game.

She learned something new about her aunt and uncle. They hadn't exactly told a lie about why they brought her to New York City, but they hadn't told her the truth either. It changed how she thought about them. She had always trusted them, even when they asked her to hand out Watchtowers and Awakes with them on Saturdays. She believed she was helping them out—that it somehow helped soothe their grief over losing Francy. But this didn't feel like that.

~

That weekend, Linda raced ahead of Ava and Charlie as they toured midtown Manhattan. The streets shimmered from the buildup of summer heat even though the skyscrapers conspired to block out the sunlight. Central Park was more to her liking. She loved how the walking paths weaved among the tall trees, and how people in summer shorts and T-shirts stretched out blankets and ate sandwiches from their picnic baskets or stared up at the sky.

"Shall we go to Macy's now?" Ava said, tucking her brown leather purse under her arm. Linda jumped up.

From Central Park, they walked block after block along Fifth Avenue, passing specialty shops with mannequins wearing fancy hats and full-length fur coats, Automats with revolving doors, enormous St. Patrick's Cathedral, and Rockefeller Center. When they passed a popular lunch place called Chock Full O'Nuts, Ava stopped.

"Let's take a break," she said.

Linda didn't recognize most of the items on the menu board. She settled for their most popular sandwich, filled with creamed cheese and chopped nuts. It wasn't her favorite cheeseburger or German hot dog, but she was too hungry to care.

~

Sunday night Ava announced that they were going to the convention early Monday morning by subway.

"See that 'X' on the map? That's where we're going tomorrow morning. It's across the Harlem River in a district called the Bronx. The concierge said it'll take us about thirty minutes to go from here to the subway stop at Yankee Stadium. That's longer than usual because of the convention. The trains will be crowded with Witnesses and with people going to work."

The subway ride felt like a cattle roundup at their ranch. When the gates closed, she was squished between her aunt and uncle, her nose lightly touching a man's starchy white shirt.

It was stuffy and warm. They stood all the way to the stadium stop, swaying as the train rolled on the tracks, and lurching each time it stopped. A half hour later, the crowd going to Yankee Stadium applauded when they arrived at the subway stop.

As they entered the stadium from a long dark tunnel, Linda saw a huge platform in the center of the field. Microphones, folding chairs, and banners strung from poles filled the platform. Someone pleaded for silence from the crowd. She trailed behind her aunt and uncle as they climbed the stairs looking for a row with empty bleacher seats for the three of them.

A man's voice, deep and resonant, bellowed over a microphone, *"Ladies and Gentlemen. Silence please. We're ready to start this proceeding."*

Linda wrung her hands together. She remembered that her grandmother had told her about her visit to New York City in the 1930s and about Anna riding her horse with Gene Autry and other stars in Madison Square Garden in 1941.

She thought about the pictures hanging in her grandmother's ranch house in the Jordan Valley. Anna looked radiant in her brilliant white cowgirl outfit, complete with chaps and a pale brown, felt cowboy hat. She was only eighteen at the time, months before she had entered the Catholic convent in Portland as a novitiate of the Holy Names sisters. Grandma Glover was proud that one of her children had chosen a religious vocation.

The crowd quieted. There were readings and singers and lots of talk about Jehovah and what it meant to be a Witness. She thought about how she had attended Catechism classes at Our Lady of the Valley Catholic Church every summer after school was out.

She remembered when she was in first grade, her cousins Nate and Eddie in the old Chevy on the drive to Ontario, timing each other to see how fast they who could say the "Our Father". They poked fun at their grandmother's habit of praying the rosary as fast as she could before Sunday Mass. Though it was an old game, Linda fell for it every time. Even at Yankee Stadium, she suppressed a giggle at the thought.

~

By the third day of the convention, Linda dreaded going on the subway. She was tired of the big crowds and the continuous talk about the Jehovah's Witnesses who led such special lives.

When they got to the Stadium, Ava bent low towards her. "Linda, honey. There's going to be a baptism ceremony today. It's a wonderful opportunity for you to be baptized. What do you think?"

Her legs suddenly turned to jelly.

"Auntie! You don't mean that, do you?" She felt like a blast of wind hit her without warning—the same kind that struck their Wyoming ranch ahead of summer thunderstorms.

"Why, of course I do. They have chartered buses to take all the people who are going to be baptized from the Bronx to Orchard Beach. Charlie and I will go with you."

Linda wished she could run away. Why was this happening? Why were her parents so far away? Why didn't Ava and Charlie tell her before the trip? They had months to discuss it with her, to ask if she wanted to convert. She remembered her mother telling her how she had converted to Catholicism before she married Dad. But her mother was twenty when she made the decision, not twelve. How could her mother's favorite aunt do this?

She jerked her head away from Ava, hoping to find space to think. But the crowd was getting noisier as they listened rapturously to the pre-baptismal talk. She needed to act quickly. There wasn't anybody around to help her escape this nightmare. She made up her mind. She wasn't going to get on a bus.

"Auntie?"

"Yes, dear?"

"I'm not going." She felt embarrassed by what she'd said. How could she defy her aunt who had taken good care of her for the past year?

Ava didn't seem to hear her in the din of the crowd. She gripped Linda's arm and pushed her toward the exit, to the gathering place outside the stadium where buses were waiting. Charlie stood tall on Ava's other side, preoccupied by the noisy crowd.

Linda shouted into Ava's ear.

"Please, Auntie. Let's turn around." She pulled down on her aunt's arm as hard as she could.

"Now, now, dear," Ava said, trying to calm her. For a moment, Linda sensed that her aunt understood her reluctance to move forward with the crowd. But Ava forged ahead. "You're already committed to Jehovah," she whispered in her ear.

Ava changed the subject. "See this? I brought your new bathing suit for the occasion!" Linda recognized it. Her aunt had purchased it for her at Macy's two days ago. Ava rummaged inside her bulging travel bag and pulled out the black and white striped one-piece swimsuit. "You'll need this for your baptism. They say there are changing rooms at the beach."

Linda shook in disbelief. She didn't hear the Bible quotes read over the mic by the speakers on stage, nor the clamor of the crowd leaving the stadium. She heard only the fast thumping of her heart, signaling her fright.

Ava nudged her forward and handed her off to Charlie. Linda clung to him as they marched in sync with the crowd. She glanced up once or twice to see what was going on in front, but there were too many people blocking her view. The crowd pushed her along. Her arms and legs felt heavy and swollen from the heat.

~

Linda couldn't count all the buses waiting outside the stadium. Someone said there were over thirty chartered to take thousands of people to Orchard Beach in Pelham Bay Park, ten and a half miles away. It wasn't long, maybe fifteen minutes, before they stepped aboard a giant bus.

They got off the bus to join a sea of people gathering at the beach. Before Ava hurried her to a portable changing tent, one of dozens set up for the special event, Linda scanned the beach. Although Charlie told her it was over a mile long, she could barely see any water. People everywhere. They reminded her of locusts swarming open fields on their Wyoming ranch in the summertime.

After changing into her new swimsuit, Linda grabbed Charlie's arm. He led her to the water's edge where men called "immersion brothers" were holding long ropes leading into deeper water. The men all wore white T-shirts and dark colored swim trunks.

"Here, honey. Grab this rope and keep wading into the water. I'll follow behind. One of the brothers will let you know when he is ready to baptize you."

She felt as clammy as the warm water swirling around her legs. She waded deeper, clinging to the heavy rope, until she felt someone touch her on the shoulder.

"What is your name, miss?" the brother asked, speaking as loud as he could over the swish of water and chatter of people.

"Linda."

"Linda, do you dedicate yourself to Jehovah?"

She wanted to cry out, "No!" but no sound came.

He smiled down at her as if she had responded affirmatively.

"Okay now, Linda, hold your breath. I'm going to immerse you in the water of Jehovah."

He grasped her shoulders tight. And like that, he pushed her backwards into the water. She felt like she was drowning. Powerless. Thrashing in the water didn't help. This man, a stranger, had total control over her. She closed her lips tight but forgot to hold her nose. Water filled her nostrils and trickled down her throat. She coughed a couple of times to clear her windpipe when her head came up for air.

Charlie shouted from behind. "I'm so proud of you. You handled that like a trooper!"

Linda looked down to her feet below the water. Her whole swimsuit was wringing wet. Her wet hair dripped to the water whirling below.

She felt wobbly as she waded back to the sandy beach. She shook every bit of the water off.

"Can we leave now, please?" she begged her uncle.

It took another two hours before they reached their hotel room. Two hours of mixing with a crowd that was jubilant over the day's proceedings. For Linda, it was the longest two hours of her life.

24

HOME AGAIN

"Take this with you, dear."

Ava handed her the shiny, brown, cosmetic case that she had taken to New York City a few days ago. Ava pressed her right hand over the hard plastic handle, making sure all of her fingers wrapped around it. It felt heavy, much heavier than on her trip to New York.

"What's in it, Auntie?"

It felt like an eternity before Ava answered her. Ava swallowed hard and looked straight at her. "*This* is our little secret, dear. The case is filled with *Awakes* and *Watchtowers*. You're a Jehovah's Witness now. But your parents won't understand that you are a special child picked by Jehovah in the last days."

Linda licked her dry lips. She couldn't taste the sweetness of the orange juice she had drunk earlier. It was a salty taste, more like after she had thrown up when she was sick with the flu earlier that spring.

Her stomach tightened. She had thought she was escaping what had happened in New York City. This was supposed to be her special day. Her father was finally coming to pick her up. She wanted to leave the Jehovah Witnesses behind. Forget the whole thing happened. But instead, she had a cosmetics case filled with the pamphlets.

Her father's booming voice filled the carport. Her heart pounded hard as she ran to greet him. He looked the same as ever—tall and handsome, though he was thinner than she remembered. He held a half-smoked cigarette in his right hand, while bending low to scoop her up with his other arm. He smiled at her. That big, broad smile that made her melt. At last he engulfed her. She wished the hug could last forever.

~

Early the next morning, she saw her father's silhouette through the kitchen doorway. He was in a hurry to leave. No smiles or friendly banter. He said goodbye to Uncle Charlie on the steps leading to the carport. Linda waved at her father with her left arm while keeping the case close to her other side, out of his sight.

"Are you ready to go, honey? We've got to get on the road."

"Coming!"

She gripped the handle tighter. Her aunt stood beside her, her back stiffened to stand taller. The natural waves of her short salt and pepper hair formed a smooth cap around her face.

The clock rang out in the living room. "Cuckoo. Cuckoo. Cuckoo..." With each cuckoo, her mind raced. It seemed like it wouldn't settle down.

She leaned down to brush her aunt's cheek with a kiss.

"Thank you for taking care of me this year, Auntie," she said, feeling grateful in her excitement. But Ava looked sad. She blotted the tears from her face and sought to hold Linda tighter.

"We'll miss you, dear."

Linda hesitated, not wanting to be unkind.

"Linda!" her father barked again from the driveway.

She wrenched herself free of her aunt's grip, spun around, and bolted for the breezeway with the case in tow.

Her father had already loaded her suitcase and some clothes boxes into the pickup bed.

"Can this case fit back there, too?" she asked.

He glanced at the load in the pickup bed. "Sure. Plenty of room."

"Here you go." She handed him the case.

"Hey. Did you put a brick in here? This thing's heavy!" He let it fall a few inches before catching it with his other hand.

She squirmed. "Just some books and papers from my school."

He peered at her. "School books?"

"Yes, Daddy." She couldn't look at him directly.

He shoved the case between some boxes. "Okay. Get in. Let's go," he said.

~

When they started the long drive up Highway 99, Linda scooted close to her father on the bench seat.

"How was your trip to New York?" he asked out of the blue.

Her heart started thumping. She'd dreaded this moment. She didn't want to tell him what happened there.

"Good, Daddy! It's a really big city, you know."

"You don't say? You mean it's bigger than Badger Basin?" He laughed. She remembered how he could make the family laugh when they were too serious about something.

"Yeah. It's a lot bigger than Badger." She felt relieved. Maybe she could forget about Yankee Stadium after all.

"Ava and Charlie said they took you to the Empire State Building. What did you think?"

She felt foolish. Of course he would have talked about the trip with them. She breathed a little easier.

"Yes. We took an elevator to the 86th floor!"

"No kidding. Did that make you dizzy?"

"No. But it went really fast, and I was afraid to look down when I got out of the elevator."

He didn't say anything else. That was more like him. Usually she was the one who asked all the questions.

"Did you see the Yankees play?" he interrupted the silence. She gulped. She wondered if Ava and Charlie said anything about going to Yankee Stadium. Or, about the convention. But baseball was his favorite game. He sometimes listened to the Yankees play on the radio at their Wyoming ranch.

"No. I hoped we could, but we didn't have enough time," she said as calmly as she could.

"Too bad. I'd like to see the Yanks play someday." He turned the radio on. "Let's see if I can find a baseball game. Maybe we can pick up the LA Dodgers since we're in southern California." He turned the dial this way and that but finally turned it off.

~

They were both quiet for a while, staring ahead at the steady stream of eighteen-wheelers and cars along Highway 99.

"How's your temporary job, Dad?" she asked. His eyes fixed on her as if she'd said something bad.

"Well, I just mean. Are you working at Uncle John's winery? Ava said that you had a temporary job and that was the reason you couldn't pick me up sooner." She hoped he might reassure her about that.

He paused. "Matter of fact, I did work for a winery cooperative last fall after the grape harvest. Your uncle helped me get the job. I got trained on how to test the sugar content of the grapes. But it was seasonal work. That's the trouble. Modesto is in an agricultural valley and most of the jobs are like that. I've been working in the orchards this summer, picking fruit. At least it's full-time work."

"That's good," she said.

"Yep," he said.

She could tell he didn't want to dwell on it, so she didn't press him further. He'd already mentioned that her mother had a secretarial job, too. How else could they rent a house?

~

As they got closer to Modesto, she thought about Christopher. Would he remember her? He was only a few months old when she last saw him. She would smother him with kisses. That would win him over. And David and Jean—would they be glad to see her? Would they resent that rich relatives had spoiled her while they were squeezed into a small house with lots of people?

Linda thought about the weeks and months that went by without any contact with her mother. Would she be excited to see her now? Why hadn't she tried to call? How could she forget her? Linda was her oldest daughter. The one her mother had relied on in Wyoming. Linda was torn between feelings of anger and excitement.

Approaching the Modesto city limits, she saw the *"Modesto"* exit signs off the freeway.

"Will Mom have dinner ready for us?"

"She sure will. Matter of fact, your mother's preparing a special meal for you."

"What is it?"

"It's a surprise. You'll have to wait and see."

She imagined a plate with meatloaf and mashed potatoes, one of her favorites.

When they pulled into the driveway around six o'clock, she wriggled to unstick her bare legs from the hot vinyl seat. Her shorts were damp from the long, hot ride through the Central Valley.

She was thrilled to see her family again. But her stomach was upset. She wished she hadn't eaten the foot-long hot dog at the Orange stand. She spotted the blocky numbers *"1308"* painted white above the front door. Her father had told her about their new neighborhood. How they had rented this three-bedroom house on Del Monte Avenue, across town from her aunt and uncle's house.

Even before Kurt honked the horn, Jean threw open the screen door. She didn't look so little anymore. Her curly brown hair bounced on the nape of her neck as she ran toward the pickup. Her dark brown eyes seemed as wide and big as her smile. She opened the side door and grabbed Linda's sweaty legs, folding her whole body over her.

"Sissy!" Jean exclaimed. "You're home!"

Linda pressed her hands on top her sister's head, reaching through her thick hair all the way to her scalp.

"Yep. I'm home."

She nudged Jean loose from her lap and swung her legs around to get out of the pickup. The rest of the family had gathered outside the truck. Her mother stood patiently, still in the clothes she had worn to her office that day—a starched white blouse and gathered cotton skirt with soft pastel flowers. She was thin, much skinnier than before, and her face was pale, almost as if she was sick.

"Hi, honey," she said, reaching through her gaggle of children to touch Linda's arm.

Linda hadn't expected her mother to be sick. She remembered how she used to get sick on holidays and family reunions. She would go to the bedroom and not come out until she felt better.

She had longed for this moment—to feel her mother's soft touch on her skin. She could smell her talcum powder, and see the hundreds of freckles on her arms and legs. It felt good to see her all dressed up, too, without her kitchen apron. She must have gotten a job like the one she had in Billings, only close to home this time. They could count on her to bring home a paycheck for their weekly grocery shopping and to pay the bills.

Baby Christopher appeared between Jo's legs. He pushed ahead to see Linda. She was astounded at how big he was.

"Christopher! You're walking!" He barely crawled when she last saw him. A flash of sadness hit her. She'd missed so much. All those growing stages babies go through.

He wiggled his little body at her.

"Leendah! Leendah!"

David or Jean must have coached him. Maybe he hadn't forgotten her after all. He was only six-months-old when she was taken to southern California. That was so long ago. Now he chortled and smiled at her. She reached down and pulled him up to her chest. He wrapped his little arms around her and snuggled his head into the crook of her neck. She trembled. He hadn't forgotten her.

"My baby Christopher," she said repeatedly.

David stepped forward as she held the baby, awkwardly swinging his right arm toward her shoulder.

"Hey, Sis. I thought you weren't going to come back from that fancy place!"

"Come on, David. You know better." She shied away from looking at him. It had been so long since they left Badger Basin together.

"Not so sure about that. Dad told us about your bedroom. How you had dozens of 45-records and a bathroom all to yourself."

She conceded his point. "I guess so. It was pretty nice."

Her mother interrupted them. "You two can talk at the dinner table. It's all set. The spaghetti and meatballs are getting cold."

Linda tried to lock eyes with her father, to ask him what happened. Had her mother forgotten that meatloaf and mashed potatoes were her favorite meal? Had she forgotten who Linda was? Kurt looked the other way as Jo herded everyone into the house.

~

When she walked through the living room, Linda noticed how bare it seemed. No thick carpet or lined floor-to-ceiling drapes in gold tones that you see in magazines featuring movie stars' homes. Only worn oak plank floors with a sofa and a round, modern-looking coffee table with some *Readers Digests* piled on top.

But she was home. She could hear the familiar din coming from the kitchen as her family sat down to supper. Chairs scooted across the wood floor; Jean tickled Christopher as she put him into his high chair.

Jean dashed from the kitchen to show her their bedroom. She pointed down the hall. "It's right there, across the hall from Mom and Dad's bedroom."

The bedroom had bare wood floors, a small, woven, wool rug next to a double bed, and a tall skinny metal medicine cabinet that served as Jean's dresser stood in the corner. Linda carefully tucked the case on a lower shelf of the cabinet and walked back to the kitchen with Jean to join the family.

After supper, her parents shuttled the kids toward the living room, holding Linda back. "We're going to have a little talk with your sister," Kurt said.

"Where?" she asked Kurt.

"On the patio. It's cooler outside."

Her mother scurried around the patio to pull together some aluminum lawn chairs for the three of them. "Here you go, honey," she said. Linda reached for the chair seat. It was still warm from the hot summer day. She gingerly sat down.

Her parents started asking her questions about her trip to New York City.

"Did you go to a Jehovah's Witnesses convention there?" her father asked.

"Daddy!" she said. "I told you about the Empire State Building, and the Hilton Hotel, and everything."

"Yes, you did. But I don't know about the 'and everything' part. Come on now, Linda. You have to tell us the truth."

Jo looked on quietly, not saying a word.

"But, Mom. What do you want to know?" Linda appealed to her mother.

Jo shifted her thin frame in the lawn chair. Her face was ashen and drawn. Her thin arms hung like dishrags on the sides of the chair. It struck Linda that her mother might be really sick. Maybe she had a serious disease. A wave of sadness suffused her. Maybe that was the real reason her mother hadn't called. But her father hadn't mentioned it today during their long trip home. Linda tried to catch her mother's eyes. But they stayed unreachable, covered by a thin watery film.

"Answer your father," Jo said firmly. "We want to know what you have in the brown case. Go get it now so we can take a look inside."

Linda's hands started shaking. "I'll have to find the skeleton key. I think it's in my suitcase."

"Fine. We'll wait out here while you get it."

She walked slowly through the kitchen and living room to the bedroom hallway. She passed by David and Jean watching TV. Christopher spotted her and cried out, "Leendah!" She acted like she didn't hear him.

When she got to the bedroom, she searched through the suitcase, still full of neatly folded clothes, to locate the skeleton key. She felt the metal key in a silky side pocket.

She pulled the brown case out of the metal medicine cabinet and trudged back to the patio. The light coming from the kitchen silhouetted her parents. She felt like a boulder was about to land on top of her.

"Okay, Daddy. Here's the case. I found the key." She pulled out the skeleton key and poked it into the hole. As she yanked the handle, the top of the case flew open, spilling issues of *Watchtower* and *Awake* across the cement patio.

"Aunt Ava and Uncle Charlie told me to bring these home and to keep them locked. They said these would help me stay a Jehovah's Witness," she whispered an explanation in haste.

Kurt stiffened. Jo was stone silent. Linda started to cry.

"Tell us what happened in New York City," her father demanded.

She began haltingly. "They told me they were taking me on a vacation. I was excited about the flight. The city was bigger than I ever imagined. Remember what I told you, Daddy? How I was afraid to look down at the crack when I left the elevator on the 83rd floor in the Empire State Building. Well, everything was like that. Tall buildings everywhere. They're called skyscrapers."

Kurt prodded her while Jo looked on. "What about Yankee Stadium? Why were you there?"

Tears brimmed in her eyes. She looked like a frightened wren.

"I got baptized there. I begged Ava not to make me. But she said I was already a Jehovah's Witness. She and Charlie took me to the big buses waiting outside Yankee Stadium. They went with me on the bus to a place called Orchard Beach. Thousands of people in swimsuits were there getting baptized. Charlie had me hold onto a long rope when I waded into deeper water until a man they called an "immersion brother" dunked me underwater. I was pretty scared."

Kurt and Jo stared at her in disbelief. They shivered in the warm night air.

"You mean you didn't know you were going to the convention before you left California?" Kurt's voice pierced the soft summer night.

"Oh, no. First time I knew was when we walked into the hotel. I saw a poster in the lobby that advertised the Jehovah's Witness annual convention in New York City. I asked Charlie. He was excited to tell me all about it." She was silent for a moment. "Aunt Ava said she told you about the trip before we left for New York."

They glanced at each other. Jo spoke up. "Not exactly. We only knew they were going to take you there this summer after school let out. They didn't mention Jehovah's Witnesses, or a convention."

~

Kurt cut short the conversation. "I think we've heard enough. There's one thing you have to do. I want you to say a rosary every night before you go to bed."

"But, Daddy. It wasn't my fault!"

"I know. But this is what you need to do." He thought saying the rosary would help get her back on track with the family. It was a familiar ritual to her at home and at the Catholic churches they used to attend.

"Mom?" she whispered, but Jo was still as a rock. Linda knew it was about penance. Penance for having done such a terrible thing. For being baptized as a Jehovah's Witness.

"There's one in the center kitchen drawer," Jo said. She didn't want to contradict Kurt's directions.

Linda went into the kitchen and rummaged through the packed drawer. She sifted through dull cutting knives, some unpaid bills, and a wad of paper napkins tucked alongside an old egg beater before spotting a rosary buried under some kitchen utensils.

"Found it!" she hollered to her parents. "Going to bed, now." She tried to understand how such a normal thing as going to bed had turned into a punishment. She walked slowly down the hall, clutching the rosary the whole way.

The light was out when she went into her and Jean's bedroom. Jean looked like she had fallen asleep. Linda started to get in next to her but decided she would sleep on the floor instead. It would be even better than just saying the rosary. It would be her way of proving to God that she hadn't given in to her aunt and uncle, after all.

She pulled a pillow from the bed and an Army blanket off the closet shelf and put them on the bare floor for the night. She clasped the rosary beads in her hand and started with the Hail Mary. *"Hail Mary Full of Grace, the Lord is with thee."* It was easy to remember. She'd said it many times before.

She slept there for several nights until Jean insisted she join her in the double bed.

"You should sleep up here."

"Never you mind, Sissy," Linda had said. "This is my idea."

It seemed a small price to pay to return home and be part of her family again.

~

Slowly, the memory of her trip to New York City began to fade. It was time to think about what it would be like going to St. Stanislaus School with David and Jean this fall. She threw the rosary beads back in the kitchen drawer the same day she folded up the army blanket and returned to the bed she shared with Jean. The old mattress was a thousand times better for sleeping than the floor.

25

THE LONG DRIVE

The three of them sat together in the last pew of the cavernous Catholic Church, waiting for Jo to begin her confession.

"Bless me father, for I have sinned," Jo began.

Linda remembered the familiar opening words, spoken quietly into the tiny window as the priest listened on the other side.

"I can hear her! Can you?" she whispered to David and Jean.

They nodded. Nothing they could do about it. They had promised their mother they would wait for her. Nearly four o'clock on a Saturday afternoon. Confessions ended at four, and they were the last to leave Our Lady of Fatima.

Linda could tell her mother was arguing with the priest because her voice kept getting louder.

"Father, how can you tell me about birth control when you've never been married? When you've never been pregnant? I know about the rhythm method. I'm living proof that it doesn't work. I have four children to feed. That's enough! I am not going to get pregnant again."

Silence filled the sanctuary. Linda nudged David. "Mom's really mad, isn't she?"

"Yep," he said under his breath. They sat like statues surrounded by larger religious icons of Jesus, Mary, and Joseph.

The priest must have muttered something to their mother. They couldn't tell what. But they knew she didn't agree with him.

"No, Father. I will not say an Our Father and three Hail Mary's for that."

He murmured something back. Moments later, the narrow confessional door sprang open, and Jo shoved it closed behind her without looking back. Her eyes found theirs. "Come on. Let's go home." That was all she said.

In fact, it was the last time that their mother went to church at all. Week after week, she found reasons not to go. During one of those times, Jo divulged her illness to Linda. "I'm doing better now, but I'm still weak from the radiation treatments I'm getting for Hodgkins. Sunday is a good day for me to get some rest."

Linda gasped. "What do you mean?"

Jo was very matter-of-fact. "It's a type of cancer. I had surgery a few months ago. Have you noticed how red my neck is?" She removed the soft cotton scarf from around her neck and drew Linda closer so she could see the deep red scar tissue adhering to a jagged line up and down the front of her neck. Linda recoiled, shaken by the horrible specter.

"Don't worry, honey. I'm getting better. These treatments are almost over. That's a good thing, don't you think?" Jo gave her a quick squeeze, as if her travails were over and done. But her mother's reassurance didn't make her feel better. Even the weak hug made her shiver. She wondered how so much had happened while she was at Ava's. She could have helped her mother, but they hadn't let her know.

~

Linda caught up with David later. "Do you know Mom has cancer?"

"Yeah, but Dad said not to scare you. He didn't tell us until after she had surgery. We just thought she had the flu or something. She's getting stronger, though."

Linda was dumbfounded. "But Mom's still going to work every day as if nothing's wrong?"

David nodded. "Guess that's the way it has to be, with Dad not having a good paying job yet. They have to pay the rent for this house, and everything else, you know."

She understood what he was saying. She was so proud of her mother for taking that stand with the priest. Linda didn't know what rhythm method meant, but her mother did, and it took courage to disagree with the priest for saying she had to do penance. But it made her sad all over again that she was living so far away from home when her mother was so sick.

~

It was August already. Kurt had enough day jobs in the orchards to keep him busy all week. He and Jo looked forward to dinner with John and Kathy on Friday night at their house. Been awhile since he'd had a chance to talk with John, and Jo hadn't strayed far from home the past few months what with her full-time job and recovery from the cancer. Having the entire family together again was both exhilarating and exhausting for her, though she never complained.

After dinner, John motioned Kurt toward the outdoor patio. "Let's go outside. We can catch the evening breeze. It's bound to give us some relief from the heat in here."

They plunked down on two Adirondack chairs shaded by the large oak tree. Their conversation was mostly about the kids, about how Linda was doing since returning from Ava's, and about Jo. John always inquired about Jo and her recovery from Hodgkins. This time was no different.

"I can't believe this, Kurt. This week, I ran into Dr. Williams at a winery event. He asked about Jo. I said we're all pleased with her progress. Then he said that one of his patients had died recently. This man had received the same experimental chemo treatment for Hodgkins, the mustard gas, as Jo. Did you know that?"

"Didn't know he died. No. But awhile back, Jo said her doctor was treating another patient with mustard gas. I haven't heard anything since. Is he worried about Jo?"

"Not so far as I can tell."

"That's good. He told us she's pulled through the worst. He attributes her recovery to strong genes and strong character!"

"He's got that right. She's a fighter," John said.

"Yep. She sure is." Kurt gazed at the freshly mowed grass, lost in thought.

"How about you, Kurt? How're you doing on the work front?"

"Not so good. The day jobs in the orchards are picking up, but I've got to bring in better wages. It's great to have Linda back, but now we've got four kids to feed, and Jo comes home worn out every night."

He didn't mention that his mother had helped with tuition so the kids could attend St. Stanislaus School this year. Even so, they barely scraped together enough cash to cover their uniforms and shoes.

"Have you thought about returning to the family ranch?"

Kurt squared up to face John. "Yep, but it's not an option. Mother has it leased out now, after Dad's death last winter. And I'm sure Sam is still opposed."

"Well, it was just a thought. You've struggled to find a job that will use your ranching skills. Given it your all. As you've discovered, there are lots of agricultural farms and increasing numbers of vineyards. Factor in an abundance of eager Mexican laborers."

"Yep. The only cattle ranches around, in the foothills, are

owned and operated by big outfits. Not a family business like I'm used to."

"I'm still rooting for you. Something good is bound to come along."

"Thanks for your support." He meant it, but he was sick and tired of having to keep reporting bad news.

Driving back home that night, the kids babbling in the back seat, they passed a used car sales lot lit up like a Christmas tree. Pole lights brightened the night sky and showed off a sea of shiny used cars. It was a special sales event intended to generate car sales in the suburbs east of Modesto.

Saturday morning, Kurt woke up thinking about the used car lot. Maybe he could get a weekend job to supplement his day labor work in the orchards. He decided to call them up. A few more dollars in his pocket every week would help.

"On the spot. Just like that." He announced to Jo with a touch of pride in how quickly he nailed the part-time job. "The manager said I could come to work next Friday night. Start the night shift at ten o'clock. Get off at seven on Saturday morning, when he reports in. I can work every Friday and Saturday night through August, when the advertising campaign ends."

"I never imagined you working in a place like that. How are you going to keep yourself awake all night? That could be your biggest challenge!"

"Aw. Don't worry about that. A few cups of java will keep me going."

Close to ten the next Friday night, Kurt left the house for his new job, but David stopped him as he reached for the car door.

"Where you going, Dad?" Kurt felt awkward about telling David. No sense in bothering the kids about his ups and downs.

"Remember that used car lot we passed on our way home from your Uncle John's last Friday night?"

"The one that was all lit up?"

"Yep. I'm going to work the night shift on Fridays and Saturdays."

"By yourself?"

"Yep. It's their end-of-summer campaign to compete with the new models. There won't be many buyers this late at night. Doesn't pay to have two salesmen there all night."

"Gosh, Dad. That sounds pretty lonely."

Kurt held up his thermos. "Your mother made some coffee for me. It'll keep me going."

Kurt waved at David and jumped into the car, leaving him standing by himself on the curb.

~

When he returned home the following morning, Linda was the first to greet him. "David told me about your new job. You look tired!"

"Yes, honey. It was a long night."

"But, Dad. A used car place?" Made her sad that her father was doing something so different from what he did on the ranch.

"Never saw myself there either. It'll help us out until I land a job that uses my ranching skills."

She had to run to catch up with him as he walked into the kitchen for some breakfast.

~

Kurt was getting used to the routine on Friday nights: check out from the orchard, drive home, have dinner with the family, put on a fresh T-shirt, and leave for Diamond Auto Sales. It had been three weeks already. He figured he must have brought home a couple hundred dollars in cash by now. Where had it gone?

That night wasn't much different from the others. No need to bring the thermos any more. They gave him an electric coffee pot and a big can of MJB. He set the coffee pot on the card table littered with promotion flyers and plugged it into a ground socket. Between the fresh brewed coffee and the bright lights, he could stay wide-awake all night.

By three in the morning, Kurt sipped his fifth cup of cheap coffee from a throwaway paper cup. He sat alone at the card table—a speck in the midst of hundreds of used cars, but no buyers around. Why would anyone stop by at this ungodly hour? He had one more weekend of these all-nighters. Then what?

This job helped out, but he still depended on Jo for steady income. Except for the hospital stay for surgery on her neck, she hadn't missed a day of work over the past eight months, even days she felt wretched from the chemo and radiation treatments. Thank God she hadn't lost her hair, too. The doctor said the dosage for the mustard gas wasn't high enough to cause hair loss.

He turned to his recent conversation with John. Ranching? Hell, yes, he missed it. Missed being his own boss, in charge of operations that changed with the season. But he'd used up his chips. Made too many poor decisions. Moved to Wyoming without checking it out first. Moved to Badger Basin, such a godforsaken place, without jobs or family around for backup. At least they had John and Kathy to help them get through this rough patch until he got a decent job. Now, this job. Another dead end.

He wondered how his mother handled the family ranch by herself. He hadn't gone back since he left the kids off last summer, though he caught up with her by phone once in a while. She said the ranch was leased out now to an outfit from Marsing. He'd never heard of them. But that wasn't so unusual. He knew all the ranchers in the Jordan Valley, but only a handful on the Idaho side of the Owyhees.

Sam crossed his mind. With the ranch leased out, would he turn his attention to other things? Hard to imagine him letting go, but he wouldn't have the excuse of overseeing the place. A hard-nosed businesswoman, their mother knew how to speak up if something wasn't done to her satisfaction.

∾

By daybreak, he'd made up his mind. When the sales manager arrived around seven, Kurt met him outside the showroom.

"'Morning, Kurt. How'd you do last night?"

"Not bad. Made two sales early in the evening. Paperwork's inside. Not much foot traffic after that."

Steve shook his hand. "Good work. Wait here a few minutes while I calculate your commissions for those sales."

"Yes, sir." Kurt was happy to oblige him. He relished having a small wad of bills pressed into his hand as payment for the night's work. It gave him a little lift before he left the lot.

When Steve returned with the cash payment, Kurt approached him. "Say. I was thinking about signing out that '56 Chevy Bel Air for a couple of days. What do I need to do?" Kurt decided to take advantage of the special perk for the used car salesmen.

"Oh. Sign your name on the clipboard, next to the key number, and write down when you'll have it back on the lot. I always ask our sales guys to return the car with a full tank, too.

"Sure will. Thanks. 'Mind if I leave my car in the back of the lot?"

"That's fine. No need to leave your keys."

Kurt had his eye on the red and white '56 Chevy Bel Air coupe. It was a beauty. He loved the big grille in front. He stuffed the bills in his pocket, unplugged the coffee pot, dumped out the stale coffee, and strode toward the coupe to get the keys.

Kurt headed north on Highway 99. He rolled down the window to catch the cool morning breeze. Wouldn't be long before the air warmed up. As the miles passed and the road signs blurred, he felt strangely exhilarated. He saw the sign for Sacramento and Highway 50 East. Figured the family would be getting up about now. They wouldn't miss him yet, so he'd keep going.

He breathed a deep sigh when he reached the Sierra foothills. Craggy live oak trees sprinkled the golden hills, daring to thrive in fields of grasses dried up by the relentless summer sun. The colorful scenery had been darkened by the night when he and Jo drove into the Sacramento Valley last summer.

A grove of manzanitas emerged on a passing hillside. The red bark and sage green leaves, along with their twisted branches, captivated him. As the highway climbed over the Sierras, the Ponderosa Pines took over. He glanced at the speedometer. He was maintaining a good speed—about fifty-five mph. He'd give Jo a call when he got into Reno. Didn't want her to be worried. The Nugget Casino on the outskirts of town was a good place to stop.

"Jo. It's me." He hollered into the pay phone to make sure she heard him. The line was quiet.

"Where are you? I thought you'd be home by now." She sounded agitated.

"I'm in Reno."

"Reno? For God's sake! What are you doing there?"

"I'm headed to the ranch. Around three this morning, I got the bug to drive there. I wanna check in with Mother, see how she's managing without Dad."

The silence seemed interminable. "Jo?"

More silence. "You there?"

"Yes." Quiet again and then Jo decided to speak. "What has

possessed you? And you're driving on those bald tires?"

"Yeah, I know. I borrowed a car from the car lot. A '56 Chevy Bel Air. Tires are in good condition. It's a perk for the salesmen. I promised to return it by Tuesday morning. I've got some cash in my pocket from the two sales I made last night."

"Oh." The phone line crackled with tension.

"I figure I can get there before dark and have all day tomorrow to visit with Mother, check out the ranch, and maybe go see my cousin, Marcus, in the afternoon. Remember him? He's still running the family ranch for Uncle Silas."

"'Course I do." She paused again. "At least you're driving a decent car. Maybe the trip will do you some good."

"What do you mean by that?"

"Lift your spirits. You've been dragging for months."

He shifted from one foot to the other, still nervous, but strangely relieved about Jo's reaction. It could have been worse. She was struggling to give him the benefit of the doubt. "Yep. It's been awhile. And I don't want to miss my work in the orchards. Look, I'll call you when I get to the ranch this evening. Would you call Mother to let her know I'm coming? I want to get back on the road."

"Okay. She'll be excited. Drive safe across that desert. Remember there aren't any cattle guards." She knew the hazards of stray cattle crossing the road in the middle of nowhere. Lots of deadly car accidents, even in the daytime.

"I'll keep an eye out."

"And, Kurt. Promise you'll never do this again. You can't leave me and the kids in the lurch like this."

"I know," he said softly, and hung up the phone.

As he drove the open desert, he felt nourished by the familiar terrain. He savored the smells of the sagebrush and delighted in the gnarly juniper trees. He reveled in the repeating patterns of dry gullies as he traveled through Nevada north to Winnemucca and by the abrupt spectacle of the Steens rising from the desert floor near the Oregon border. He thought about new possibilities for himself. Maybe he shouldn't have given up ranching altogether.

He reached McDermitt, Nevada at four o'clock, buoyed by his progress. McDermitt was only a spot in the road, but the historic stagecoach town straddled the Nevada-Oregon border, marking his final leg home. Fewer than a hundred miles to go. His head buzzed from fatigue, but he looked forward to seeing his mother again.

≈

A short nap revived him. He and his mother spoke into the night. She swayed gently in her old rocker, and he perched upright on a wooden kitchen chair polished smooth from years of use.

"You'll see for yourself, Kurt. This Dan McGraw outfit isn't taking good care of this place. They stop by during the week to do the essentials. Otherwise, they stay away."

"That's terrible! I'm gonna check things out in the morning, Mother."

She patted his hand. "Good. Glad you're here. Now, how about you? Have you landed a job that suits you?"

"It's been tough. I never expected to be working as a day laborer in orchards and, lately, selling used cars on weekends. I haven't found anything that lets me use my ranching experience."

Her taut face gave away her disappointment. "That's too bad. Surely, something will come along soon?"

"Hard to say. John asked if I'd considered returning to run

this ranch. He knows I've struggled to secure a decent job in the agricultural industry of the Central Valley."

"He did?"

"Yep. He brought it up. I told him I wasn't considering it. That you have it leased now, and Sam might object. Besides, John knows I swore off ranching again after Wyoming."

The mention of Sam reminded him.

"What is Sam up to these days? What does he think about your leasing this place?"

"You knew he moved to Boise last fall? He passed the exam for his real estate license, and decided he would do better there than here. He and his family live in a new development on the outskirts of Boise. He seems to be doing pretty well for himself."

"No kidding?" Kurt couldn't believe it. He'd never imagined that Sam might actually move that far from the valley and leave his gas station business.

"Does he still talk about getting the ranch someday?"

"He hasn't said anything about that for a long time. He's too busy with other things these days. He called me earlier today, his weekly call. I told him you were on your way. He was pretty surprised."

Kurt squirmed in his chair, suddenly feeling uncomfortable. He might have to drive to Boise to see his brother. He was determined to see him before returning to California.

His mother got up slowly from the rocker. "Well, Son, it's past my bedtime."

"Mine too. It's been a long day. Have a good sleep."

Kurt watched as she lumbered to her bedroom. She had always been on the heavy side, but with the energy of a thirty-year-old. Now, for the first time, he was glad her bedroom was downstairs so she wouldn't have to negotiate those steep stairs.

～

Kurt woke early on Sunday morning to walk the ranch. He opened doors to every building still standing, including the three-seat outhouse that his family had used until they added an indoor bathroom, in 1936. He was in high school then. The weathered old barn was still a shelter for the horses during the wintertime. Its roof was in fair condition. At least it wasn't caved in like the storage shed or falling down like the corral. The deteriorating condition of these support structures distressed him. The McGraw outfit sure wasn't maintaining the place.

As he came out of the barn, still smelling a mix of dusty old hay and dried manure strewn helter-skelter on the floor, he noticed a small John Deere utility tractor parked outside the double doors. True to form, a key was stuck in the ignition. It was too good an opportunity. He swung onto the metal seat and took off for the fields.

The drive through the first big alfalfa field, freshly mowed in long narrow rows, reminded him of the sweet days of summer on the ranch. He stopped the tractor and listened to the cacophony of sounds—the grasshoppers on the ground, the blackbirds soaring overhead, and the riffles of Jordan Creek close by. It intoxicated him. He felt in touch with the land again. His land.

Kurt found the narrow path leading across the creek. He dipped the tractor downhill to the shallow streambed, fending off willow branches until he entered the fields on the west side. He hopped off, inspected the crop, and scanned the surrounding fields. His mother was right. The McGraw outfit lagged behind where they needed to be to get the standard two cuttings during the season. Some years they could count on three. That would provide them a healthy income. They must not be hiring the help they needed to get the job done quicker.

Something rustled near the stream. He turned around to locate the sound. A man shoved his arm through the thick cluster of willows bordering the creek trail. Kurt recognized his brother walking toward him.

"Sam!"

He looked like a businessman from the city, dressed in a crisp white short-sleeved shirt and khaki trousers with knife-edged creases that looked strangely incongruous with the soaking wet cuffs. He clutched his oxfords in one hand.

"Yep. It's me. Had to wade through the creek to find you. I heard the tractor. Mother said you were out here."

Kurt stepped back, stunned by Sam's unexpected appearance. "Surprised to see you out here. So you're selling homes now in Boise. How do you like it?"

Sam set his shoes carefully on the field stubble. "It's a whole lot better than changing tires and pumping gas."

"Good for you," Kurt intoned.

"Yeah. How about you? What brings you to the ranch?"

"Wanted to check up on things since the McGraw outfit took over. It's been over a year since I came through here on my way to California. If you count the three years Jo and I were in Wyoming, it's been over four years since I've walked these fields."

"Mother must have told you the McGraws have leased the place. No need for you or me to second-guess how they operate it. The important thing is, Mother doesn't have to worry about it anymore. She's got guaranteed income so long as they carry out the lease provisions."

"Yeah. I'm aware of all that. With Dad gone, Mom's been carrying a big load. She made a wise decision to get it leased out."

Kurt wasn't sure if he should say more. Whether he should go into how the ranch had deteriorated. And he wasn't about to tip his hat to his possible return to ranching.

"So you're in California. I hear the wine industry is growing like crazy, and there are plenty of good jobs for Aggies. What have you lined up for yourself?"

Sam still knew how to get under his skin. He felt his face flush.

In California, 'Aggie' was shorthand for the Central Valley's rich agricultural heritage. But Sam's choice of words and derisive tone mocked Kurt's love for ranching. It took him back to the annual Christmas party at Clark School when Mickey Olmsted belittled him for moving the family off the ranch to Badger Basin. His words echoed in his mind,

"You never learned how to make a living off your land. If you had, you wouldn't be working as a ranch hand at Fraker's place over the winter."

He had wanted to knock Mickey out that night. That's what he deserved. But he had Jo to protect—she was eight months pregnant—and wedged between the two men. So he had resorted to calling his adversary "difficult" and walking away.

Kurt glared at his brother. "I've learned a few things about the wine industry. Like I've learned how to calibrate the sugar content of the grapes at harvest time. That's a technical skill most ranchers don't have. But that's not what I love to do."

Sam shuffled closer so he could stand nose-to-nose with Kurt. "What is it you love to do? As far as I can tell, you haven't done very well in running ranches."

"What do you know about it, Sam? I took some risks I shouldn't have. I've learned some things the hard way. Apparently you haven't noticed the McGraws are letting this place go to hell. They're way behind in the summer cuttings. And many of the buildings are in bad need of repair. The corral, too, for that matter."

Sam dug in. "What are you trying to tell me? Surely, not that you want to manage the ranch again?"

"Actually, I'm giving it some thought. I know how to run this place. Years of experience under my belt. Why should I keep hitting my head against the wall in California, where ranches are heavily mechanized operations on thousands of acres, not suited to someone like me with single-family ranching background. It's a different ballgame."

"You can't afford to buy that size spread anyway."

"'Course not."

"You'd be a fool to return, Kurt. Mother's better off with the McGraws than she would be with you."

"You're full of baloney, Sam. I can do a heck of a lot better job than that outfit. They're running it into the ground. This is obviously just a side operation for them. Besides, there's nothing you can do if I decide to come back."

Sam's face contorted in anger. "You'd better think twice about it."

Sam bent over to put on his shoes. He twisted around. "Hate to ask you for a ride back."

"Stand here," he said, pointing to the tractor step. He pulled the throttle and headed toward the creek.

~

After dropping Sam off, Kurt drove eight miles north of town to visit his cousin, Marcus. The Silas Glover ranch was a huge enterprise with thousands of acres. The original three-story ranch house matched the splendor of the spread, with a grand staircase to the second floor, and a schoolroom adjacent to the teacher's living quarters on the top floor. Marcus's grandfather had married the young schoolteacher who came from the East Coast many years ago. Two other homes, built in recent decades, formed the current family compound.

The two cousins had always liked each other. Kurt recounted his fresh observations about the ranch. "What do you think, Marcus? Mother needs to turn this around before the season becomes a disaster."

They brainstormed the possibilities. At one point, Marcus asked the obvious. "What about you? Any chance you could take over?"

Kurt fumbled for words. "After losing the ranch in Wyoming a couple years ago, I vowed I'd never operate a ranch again."

Marcus pressed him on this. "Understandable. But haven't things changed since your dad died?"

"Funny thing. I said it out loud for the first time today when Sam showed up out of the blue. He drove over from Boise to see what I was up to. He had a lot of gall. Demanded to know why I was visiting. Worried that I might be planning to return. I told him I was thinking about it."

"You did?!"

"Yep. I hadn't planned on it. This trip was my desperation move. I had to get out of town. Clear my head. But it has made me think about running the ranch again. As you say, things have changed on the folks' ranch, and I can't continue doing what I'm doing in California."

"I'm sure you've taken your lumps, so have I, but your love of ranching runs deep. It's in our blood. I bet your father would be proud to have his son back on the ranch. I can help you make it a going concern again."

"My God, Marcus. I don't know what to say. Thanks. It would be such a big deal for my family. Jo doesn't have any inkling, so I'd have to talk with her. And of course, Mother."

Marcus shrugged his shoulders, backing off a little for Kurt's sake. "It feels like the time is right. I'll be glad to help if you decide to return. No question you'll succeed, so long as you want to do it."

Kurt paced the room. "I'll talk with Mother tonight. Find out more about the lease. See if she truly likes the idea. Then there's Jo. I'll talk to her when I get back home."

Marcus clasped Kurt's hand. "Good man!"

When he arrived home, his mother was sorting through fresh ears of corn from her side yard. "Mother, I've got to talk with you."

She pulled the apron over her head and tossed it aside. "Sit down. We can talk right here."

They slid onto the wood bench that bordered the corner of the kitchen.

"From what I saw today, the McGraws are running this place into the ground. They should be on the second mowing by now, but they're still working on the first. My guess is they haven't hired enough help, or they aren't putting in enough time. Either way, it could spell disaster for you this fall."

She didn't flinch at the bad news.

"I talked with Marcus. He'll give me backup if I need it. With Dad gone, he wants to help out family. What do you think if I were to take over in the short term? There's the lease, of course. When does it terminate?"

"December 31st. Only four months away."

"Too bad it's not next month. Even the end of September would be better."

"Why don't you let me work that out with the McGraws? I could buy out the remainder of the lease. There's a provision for that. You never know. They might be grateful for the reprieve. Main thing is I'd love to have you back managing the place. You have the know-how and the energy. We can work something out that gives you the income you need for the family."

Kurt leaned across the table and grabbed his mother's hands. "Thanks, Mother." His grin was as wide as the bell jar on the table.

"I know. It's been a rough road for you. Now you can get a new start."

"I'll talk with Jo soon as I get home. Get her reaction. She'll be surprised, but I expect she'll warm to the idea."

"Hope so, Son."

~

Kurt returned the car to the sales lot late Monday afternoon, ahead of schedule, and with a full tank of gas.

The kids were all over him moments after he walked through the living room door. Jo gave him a peck on his cheek and retreated to the kitchen.

"We missed you," Linda said as she stroked his arm. "How's Grandma?"

"I missed you guys, too." He flashed a big smile at the kids circled around him. "Grandma's doing fine. I told her all about your shenanigans and how much you've grown. She sends her love."

They jostled for position to tell him about their weekend.

"I biked to St. Stanislaus yesterday with Jean and David," Linda chirped. "Clear across town, Dad! Took us about half an hour to get there."

"Good for you! What did you think about the school?" he asked.

"It's really nice. I can hardly wait till school starts."

"Yeah, Dad. That was the first time that Linda has biked across railroad tracks and she didn't even flinch," Jean piped up.

Kurt grinned at Jean. "I'm not surprised. She's going to be a veteran biker like you and your brother before long."

But he kept thinking about what Linda had said about going back to school. Where had the summer gone? August, already.

"I'm fixing up a used Schwinn, Dad," David proudly announced. "I need to return Anthony's bike before school starts."

"Is that so! Where'd you get the bike?"

"One of the kids down the street, name's Jon Cook, gave it to me. It's his old bike. He's got a bigger one now, so he doesn't need it. It had a flat tire, but I patched the hole. I'm going to add a kickstand and it'll be like new."

They talked non-stop for quite a while. The girls assured him they had helped their mother with the dishes at night. It was one of their daily chores, but they wanted to get some mileage out of it since Kurt had been gone almost three days and they knew he was concerned about Jo building up her strength from her illness.

He waited until the kids were in bed before talking with Jo. She still had a burr under her saddle about his trip.

"I can't figure out what got into you, Kurt. Why'd you take off without talking with me first? Totally unlike you!"

"Now, Jo. Sorry you're upset." He wrapped his arm around her waist, but she shoved it away.

"Sitting on that folding chair last Friday at three in the morning surrounded by used cars, I was struck by the hole I'd dug for myself. Maybe it was the clear summer night sky, or too many cups of stale coffee, but I realized that with two part-time jobs, I'm on a road to nowhere."

He detected a twinge of annoyance. Or was it sympathy? He couldn't tell which. Jo was so thin now—she must have lost twenty pounds—he wanted to protect her from any harm. But damn if he hadn't done the opposite!

"Well, you don't gain anything by running away from your troubles, even though it was to your folks' ranch. I hope the road trip did you some good. I know how you love to drive the high desert."

"You're right. No doubt about it. There's something in the landscape that inspires me. The open skies. The Steens jutting from the Alvord. Beautiful country."

Jo lightly stroked his arm, momentarily forgetting her upset. "That's one of the things I love about you."

"But maybe there's a silver lining to this whole thing. I've got a plan."

"A plan?"

"Yep. Remember how that outfit from Marsing has a lease on the ranch?"

She nodded.

"Well, they're running the place into the ground. They're behind on haying, barely into the second cutting. Makes it unlikely they'll get a third before fall. And the buildings are in bad shape. Mother said the workers show up only a few days a week--"

"So what did you recommend?" Jo interrupted. "That your mother end the lease early?" He could tell she was thinking about how they faced the same threat in Wyoming. It still felt painful.

"Yes, sort of. I offered to take over from them if Mother can terminate the lease before December 31st. She liked the idea. Matter-of-fact, she offered to contact the McGraws herself and see if they might be okay with it. She thinks they might 'appreciate a reprieve,' as she put it."

"What about Sam? Did you talk to him about your plan?"

He smiled broadly. "Sure did. Though I didn't expect to blurt it like I did. He was being his usual surly self. Saying things like how the McGraws could take better care of the place than me. And he called me an Aggie—not in the California way."

"Sounds like Sam alright!"

"Yeah. But I didn't let him get away with it. About time, I guess. Told him if I decide to come back, he can't stop me."

She grinned. "You did? Good for you!" She paused again. "You mean you would go there by yourself for a few months? Or are you thinking the whole family would move back?" Suddenly, she had that oh-my-god look on her face.

He glanced down, hoping to buy some time. "I know it's complicated, but I want you and the kids to move there with me. Our whole family."

He'd just seen the kids' excitement about starting school next month. Like him, they had plans for their future. He felt their enthusiasm for city life. They were settling in as a family again after two long years.

He forged ahead anyway. "It's the best chance I have to get us on a solid financial footing again. Mother promised to work it out so we have the income we need for the family. As Marcus said about my love for ranching, 'It's in my blood.'"

As if watching a movie, Jo stayed quiet. She simply stared at Kurt and nothing more.

He threw in the trump card. "This'll give you a chance to get off the roller coaster of working for the law firm. Remember how you thrived on the Wyoming ranch? You worked hard, no question, but the kids were our big helpers. All three pitched in to save the bummer lambs, and you taught the girls how to plant that huge garden and can the vegetables each fall. Remember how David was my right-hand man in the fields? I bet they'd jump at the chance to do those things again."

He sensed her stubborn discomfort rubbing against his dream.

"Kurt! I can see how much this means to you," Jo said, finally breaking her silence. "Getting back to ranching again, and on your folks' place. But how can we do that? It isn't the right time for the family. Our kids are finally together again, and they feel good about living here. Linda is still adjusting from her year with Ava and Charlie. She's excited about going to St. Stanislaus with David and Jean this fall."

Her skepticism hit him in the gut, but her words rang true. "I can't do this, Kurt. Not another big move. I don't have much strength for routine work, let alone packing and making moving arrangements. And where would I find a cancer specialist in that part of the country?"

That hit him hard. "I know what you're saying, Jo. Let me think about it." It was clear that he couldn't pack up the kids and

Jo and move them wholesale to eastern Oregon. Not the same as previous moves. Jo's illness had to be considered, and the kids were growing up. They had their own opinions about things now. Yet he hadn't felt this hopeful in a long, long time.

He looked up at her. "Let's talk with the kids about this tomorrow."

She hesitated. "So long as we talk about the whole situation as a family—our jobs, my recovery."

He said nothing, but then a smile brightened his face. Convinced that together they could figure a way forward, Kurt took Jo's hand.

THE END

ACKNOWLEDGMENTS

I am deeply grateful to my family, friends, and colleagues who have provided encouragement, professional critique, and wise counsel along the way:

My son, **Matthew Silas**, camera and staging artist at Pixar, for his tenacious belief in the value of this story from the outset, and for his professional assistance on the writing, book cover design, and readying the manuscript for publication.

Thank you as well to **Quyen Tran**, award-winning cinematographer for Matt's short film, The Fence, at the 2008 UCLA Film Festival, for graciously allowing me to use a photo from that film on the book cover.

My mother, **Marcia Skinner**, for reading multiple drafts of many chapters and answering my questions about ranch life in the 1950s. Likewise, thanks to my brother, **Tim Skinner**, for retelling stories about his boyhood on ranches in the West, and to my sister, **Barbara Allen**, for her enthusiastic support and vivid personal anecdotes.

My editor and award-winning novelist, **Robbi Sommers Bryant**, for her stellar developmental and copy editing of the manuscript. Likewise, to **Caroline Leavitt,** noted author and instructor at the UCLA Extension Writers' Program, who provided invaluable editorial advice on an initial draft.

Sincere thanks as well to my academic colleagues for their generous advice and consultation: **Maxine Chernoff**, poet and chair of the Creative Writing department at San Francisco State University; and **Lynda Swanson**, former campus planner for

Stanford, UC San Francisco, SF State University, and the Oregon University System.

I am also indebted to the ***2014 Napa Valley Writer's Conference***, most especially the fiction-writing workshop led by author ***Ayana Mathis***. And to workshop attendees/authors, ***Shelley Blanton-Stroud*** and ***Dorothy Rice***, for their dedicated advocacy and support.

And a special thanks to my husband, ***Bob Lanier***, who has served as my sounding board and first-editor during every stage of the writing.

ABOUT THE AUTHOR

Marilyn Skinner Lanier is the offspring of Oregon pioneers going back to the 1860s. Raised on cattle ranches in eastern Oregon and northwest Wyoming before moving to California in the late 1950s, the author draws on familial material to dramatize the emotional upheaval of an American family caught in the cultural transition from the rural West to exploding urban America after World War II. This is Ms. Lanier's first novel. She lives in Sonoma County with her husband. They are the parents of five adult children.

@lanierMarilyn

https://facebook.com/marilynskinnerlanier

www.linkedin.com/marilynskinnerlanier

www.marilynskinnerlanier.com